About the Author

Born in North Carolina in 1995, William Cameron Edge graduated from the University of North Carolina at Chapel Hill in 2018 with a bachelor's degree in linguistics and religious studies. Outside of writing, he spends a significant amount of his time learning languages.

Quotidian Drag

William Cameron Edge

Quotidian Drag

Olympia Publishers
London

www.olympiapublishers.com
OLYMPIA PAPERBACK EDITION

Copyright © William Cameron Edge 2023

The right of William Cameron Edge to be identified as author of this work has been asserted in accordance with sections 77 and 78 of the Copyright, Designs and Patents Act 1988.

All Rights Reserved

No reproduction, copy or transmission of this publication may be made without written permission.
No paragraph of this publication may be reproduced, copied or transmitted save with the written permission of the publisher, or in accordance with the provisions
of the Copyright Act 1956 (as amended).

Any person who commits any unauthorized act in relation to this publication may be liable to criminal prosecution and civil claims for damage.

A CIP catalogue record for this title is available from the British Library.

ISBN: 978-1-80439-474-8

This is a work of fiction.
Names, characters, places and incidents originate from the writer's imagination. Any resemblance to actual persons, living or dead, is purely coincidental.

First Published in 2023

Olympia Publishers
Tallis House
2 Tallis Street
London
EC4Y 0AB

Printed in Great Britain

Dedication

This book is dedicated to Bishop Harry and Trey Autry.

Acknowledgements

Thank you to Dr. Lisa Aldred for helping me find the confidence to put these words to paper and for her suggestions on early drafts.

1

Well, I stooped down and offered my hand to the fiddler crab. He stared back at me in numinous silence.

"We're pals, right?" He obliged me with his firmest grip. I yelped, ripping my finger free of his brittle sea talons. He scuttled off to his tunnel. "I understand, my friend! Until better times!" I shouted after him, resting my hand in a passing wave. I rose and meandered up town's way. Exuberant flows of sea oats waved me along as sand pushed into the gaps of my toes. Life-loving spurs kissed the soles of my feet.

"Forgive us, for we know not what we do!" they screamed as they slid up to the hilt. I stopped here and there to toss them aside. My stomach steered me on, grumbling as the sun slipped behind the tide. I smiled and yawned with the great horizon. It had been a good day. What day it was, I couldn't say. The moon kept its frothing waters at bay, and I spoke a word of gratitude for its sake. My stomach repeated its demand for an offering. I took a right at the road for the pier.

I slid my calloused fingers along the chipped black bike rack by Vinny's Pizza Shack. There was a young scarecrow swaying by the door. There wasn't a trace of joy in his eyes to show for the eighty bucks of liquor sloshing in his gut. His chin drifted with the course of the river over the darkened bridge to his feet. Neither he nor I could afford to ignore the return of the sun. I sauntered up to the entrance. Whose reflection did I see in those parting glass doors? I tried not to seem unpresentable on purpose.

"*SHIRT*," half-shouted the barkeep. Just then I noticed the breeze stinging my back. I reached to feel a seashell's fresh cut and the neat sting of seawater and sand seeping into the human artifact. Where the hell was my shirt? I nodded and turned away, a scruffy aperture of nature's horrified self-knowledge bumbling by with the cackling gulls.

"Frittered away, frittered away," I mumbled. I straightened my back in a plea for dignity as my mane blew into my face. Shoving hands into my pockets, I noticed my shirt soaked and sandy deep within. I took a moment to admire the shapeless mess in my hands, glittering with sandy little jewels. I turned my back to the waterway and peeled the doors open vested with the confidence of any standard issue consumer. My drained acquaintance nodded reluctantly, knowing he was to lower me into the gloom of the whiskey well.

Vinny's broke even during the summer floods of tourism and dried up to the gills every other season of the year, except at the oyster festival in the dead of winter. An exhausted skeleton crew tended to its electric bulk in the hospice days of spring's final chill. Maybe someone snoring on an old fishing boat down the waterway could remember its analog glory days in the mid-eighties, if someone somehow cut the beer drip cocooning their mind in its fragile suspension of chaos. Until then, a sea squirt would know Sassoon better than anyone alive. I was surprised to see the pizza oven still slowly imploding in a dim corner reflecting the light of flatscreens playing absolute dreck from open till close. The visionary new direction undertaken by the sculptors of Vinny's headstone had taken his life's work to the heart of an imaginary mainstream. When it washes up in shards on the shore, the best of it will have been rotting in the dump for centuries.

Sassoon was at the head of an obscure southerly archipelago

bobbing nigh imperceptibly off the coast of North Carolina. I mean just off the coast, separated only by a snaking waterway flowing between the two domains. The paradise beyond the shore blossomed with flooded forests, crowded wetlands, and brackish ports. From the sea, the islands were like coins on a coffee table straining for a separate existence from the abyss. The drains on the sides of the cracked and empty roads sat below sea level. All roads eventually ended in a smothered passage into a crowd of dunes.

Our island was a mottled smattering mashed together by concrete and the encroaching sea. There were more homes than trees. Half of these were empty most of the year. Some plants were of course invited to exist outside of nature's evaporating tidal pool so long as they didn't chew the scenery or block billboards. Mushrooms were meticulously expunged from the poor soil. Any freshwater feeding the shrinking scrub of the marginal dune territories between the beach and the road came by the grace of heaven.

Most of the people who worked on the island could only afford to live on the mainland over the bridge. They commuted to serve among empty homes that continued to rise in price despite the sandbags crowding around their barnacle infested stilts. The beach was on life support, besieged by time. I looked at a black and white photograph of ol' Vinny with his pudgy button face and a still-faint saintlike twinkle in his eye. The new owners may not have shared his tastes, but at least they kept his fleshy face around.

"Can I see some ID?" asked the bartender. I pulled mine out of a salt-blasted shell of a wallet and showed him. I was almost certain he'd seen me twenty-eight of the last thirty nights, almost. Policy was policy, of course, and far above the fallen logic of the world. "All right Jedediah, what'll you have?" he asked, sliding my identity back to me. My heart sank into my gut as my eyes met his. What would he rather be doing? I asked him his name once and forgot. I asked again and forgot again, so the great farce goes.

"Absofuckinglutely," I replied. There was an acute silence. The dude kneaded his brow while squeezing air between his teeth. I turned to see a family of seven just in and famished from the beach. The white-haired matriarch gave me the evil eye. I dipped my head.

"So… What'll you *have?*" he asked.

"What?" I stiffened. He searched my eyes for signs of life. "Uhhhh… Can I get that amber ale over there?" He slid his finger over a row of labels, waiting for a nod.

"When was the last time I drank sober?" I thought. The room felt empty all of a sudden.

"We'll pray for you son," said the matriarch as she shut the door. The long-suffering son of the sea cracked a bottle and set it before me. I was touched at the offer of a prayer. That withering look, was it really one of contempt?

I finished my drink and asked for another, pointing at random. He handed me an IPA. The label sported a family of Gothic cannibals turning human intestines into sausages. It was quite a departure from the film noir vignette plastered over the last one.

"It's from a local brewery. You can tell they toned down the aftertaste," said the bartender.

"That's an… interesting label."

"It sells," he shrugged.

The beer's saccharine downpour whisked me away to the great distillery within. I set another empty bottle on the bar and looked at the clock. Hours had passed. I wondered how many I still had to waste. I asked for another.

"Maybe I amused someone today," I thought. I tilted the bottle back, ignoring a screaming voice inside calling me a waste of space. My journey home would be a fair trek in the rain. There could be no giving up halfway. The voice cared, and it may have been right at the time, but I had to value my life or lose it to exposure. It's dangerous to weigh a human life like a fat sack of gilders. I scoured my memory for proof of contribution. I blathered until I was finally drunk enough to ask the gentleman his name.

"It's Sep. It's also last call. Any more soliloquies before you walk home?" he asked. Without looking away from the clock I mumbled:

"They always tell you to be yourself. They never tell you that who you become might end up being the problem. I was in love once. I never thought that would be the problem with me."

"...Wow, well it's about time we get her prepped and closed."

"*Time*... I bet she's doing *really* well," I mumbled.

"49.97, cash or card?" I slid another battered piece of plastic to him and chewed off a piece of my lip. I stared out into the middle distance like a lamb waiting for a sliver of silver to cut the universal veil. I signed and made for the door. I was impressed, ripped as I was, that I was still able to put one foot in front of the other. The sea breeze picked up and speckled my cheeks with drops of frigid water as the cars driving by showered my shoes. I heard a voice calling out to me.

"You forgot your card!" My exhausted acquaintance didn't have to run far to find me.

"Fuck, sorry man..." I mumbled and stumbled leaning in to snatch my identity back from his waiting hand.

"Be good."

"Yeah." I imbibed the aroma of several quintillions

spawning and dying in the waters lapping over the stilts and yards and yawning up into the stars. There were hints of exhaust in the mix, a few dozen dinners too, and meteorites of asphalt poking out of the sand. I could hide the most obvious tell that I was sinking below the power of speech by keeping my mouth shut, but what about my slurred eyes and glazed gait? I knew I would not remember the coming hour. The moon of the afternoon beamed like a knife hovering over the fire, our generous ration of sunshine for the night. I felt terror and joy in the prospect that I might never salvage what was left of me. Headlights passed in the rain. Streetlamps illuminated patches of sand and their weeds of paradise. Some of the lights flickered tenuously. Enunciation of any but the simplest kind required minutes of rehearsal.

I produced a sample of an unknown tongue for the apprehension of a passing lab: "Rubuwan, abuvad udenem?" The sweet dog licked his lips strained against the leash to look me in the eye, beckoning me to transmit the message in full. The gentleman walking him nodded at me and walked stoically by, afraid to provoke a potentially litigious stranger.

Spring left the moment it arrived, nudged out by the year's great summer. I found my way home after a few wrong turns. The house was a one-story deal on stilts with a lovely little staircase clattering up to a screen door. I'd received it from an entomologist uncle who'd gone to live under a geodesic dome with a flock of geese and a whippet named Arnold. I wondered who'd become the bigger eccentric.

The moment I slumped back onto the couch I nearly lost consciousness. Every time I closed my eyes, I could feel my mind slip out through the top of my skull and spill out onto the cushions. Was that the angel of death I heard rummaging around the other room? I bolted up and searched the house. I shoved stacks of old hand-drawn comics in the closet aside half hoping

I'd find him and finally extract some kind of explanation. I sat empty in my tub with the shower on, for protection. It was essential that I stay awake in order to survive. I woke up frozen through.

I wrapped myself in blankets and paced around my grotto searching for a hint of warmth in jumbled family photographs. I sat down to write some bleary apology. As I scraped ash and books aside to make room for my letter, it all came together. The heaviness in my handwriting accused me of laying things on too thick. The skew of my letters betrayed a wavering grasp on my nerves. Their inconsistency, *s's* that looked like *g's* and *g's* that resembled *a's*, indicated that I suffered from a severe lack of discipline.

All I remember thinking about was whether I would catch pneumonia. Not a trace of my broken heart materialized on that paper, stricken over with ink. 'Sorry' did not make it either. When a little stillness emerged from the bleak malaise, I meditated for what felt like an hour on the porch. All the while it was consciousness of nausea, recognition of nausea, despairing over nausea, frightening myself about nausea, having perfect contentment with nausea, and throwing up. I opened my eyes and saw a spider cricket on the panes of my shuttered window, munching away at an ant pilfered from the Earth. I smiled. I was happy.

Terry, an old friend from high school, texted to say he was coming back from a long sojourn in the west out of nowhere. He wanted to come and visit me. It was cool if I said no. He had plenty of offers. He just missed me. I smiled at that. Terry was an artist at heart, his canvas was the ground beneath his feet. His performance as himself was as flawlessly conducted as it was completely unpredictable. I couldn't imagine surviving what he had. Apparently, at the end of a harrowing season in Bakersfield, he and a large chunk of change had been parted. I wondered who in the noise music community could have masterminded his downfall.

"Not to worry, of course. That's all right now. Wallace helped me."

"Well... That's very good. Come on over. We'll pull corks." I told him if he needed me, I was there. Wouldn't you? He floated the idea of maybe staying for two nights.

"Make a weekend of it," he said. I acquiesced.

I went to the bathroom, turned on the light, and looked in the mirror. I saw someone I was never supposed to see. I tried to be positive about the damage I'd done, but I was genuinely scared. I looked into my eyes and saw only the appearance of youth. Only a year before, I was someone else. I didn't see that person in those eyes. I thought to myself that I didn't have to feel so old and worn out if I only quit drinking. Why did I need poison? Resolving to forget the painful truth, I sank into the seabed and let the amber waves take my lights away.

***

I woke up with the sun in my eyes. My polluted veins pulsated with the gulls and fish basking in the bane of my tainted eyes: the nectar of sunshine. I was on the porch again. I slumped down at my kitchen table and was just rolling up a fat cone for the hangover when Jeremy called. He was applying lipstick over the line and enunciating marvelously despite the fact. Eventually I was compelled to interrupt his retelling of his reign over a dreamland of gnomes and the political conspiracy that led to his unjust expulsion to move a bag of garbage leaning against my thigh. I grabbed the bag and ambled over to the kitchen, afraid that the horrible mass of glass and soured beer inside might go spilling all over the floor. With the sweet, intolerable stench of the booze now appropriately far enough away from my workstation I returned to my phone.

"Hit me."

"Yeah, so afterwards I go to *work* and Gabriela and I are hanging out behind the counter, shooting the shit, and out of nowhere she asks if I wanna partake of some DMT."

"No shit? What happened?" I took a quotidian drag while scratching a mosquito bite. Apparently, I wasn't alone after all.

"I took her up on the offer, what else?"

"Did anything try talking to you?" I asked. He smiled.

"I gotta tell you face to face."

"You really called me to tell me all about your secret life as a gnome despot? With a juicy interdimensional odyssey like that stuck between your ears? It's no secret you do drugs, Jeremy. Your FBI agent's heard all your confessions. What's to lose?"

Jeremy paused to breathe, maybe to look up at the sky or into one of his paintings. "There just aren't many words you could hang on an experience like that. It's like one moment I hated certain people, the next I didn't hate anything." Except for the sea and its endless fuckery, there was silence on the line. "Stay high and dry friend," click.

I took the roach from my lips and started rolling another, flicking the first into a corner. Another crawled over my hand. An impulse to flatten him fast against the varnished wood went through me. I raised my fist and the senseless anger passed like a summer rain. I had to get away from my desk. Nothing ever got done there but I still managed to destroy my life there several times. I paced around the room as the sun made its rounds. I sensed the reality of Earth's perilous plummet through the void as my own, covered up by a sunny afternoon. I peered across the canal through the blinds of my rear window. There was a big gent in a moth-eaten hat in his yard stooped over his grill with domestic brew in hand. The scene's idyllic simplicity reminded me somehow of the early aughts. It was not an idyllic or simple time, but it was when boats littered Sassoon's canals, before a great many people were foreclosed on and the island emptied out. It was when people could afford to remain where they were born, more or less.

I thought of all the giddy folks who'd roar out to the gulf stream at dawn with a suitcase of beer to wrestle with creatures of the deep. The brownish-blue waters shimmered in their multitudes: croakers, mahi, king mackerel, dogfish, marlin. Out swimming, myriad claws, stingers, and the silt-blinded schnozzes of tiger sharks are never too far. How deep and vast and fucking opaque is the sea!

As the great machine began breaking apart in a race to outpace itself the boats grew smaller and scarcer. The Henderson's patties hissed in the noonday sun, spitting grease. Their kids ran around in the yard. Young Arlo seized his foot in hand and hopped on the other. Sam went over there to see what was the matter. Sand spurs know neither friend nor foe. I blew smoke off the windowpane. It could have been fire ants, solenopsis invicta, the jealous champions of lawns and median strips. He wasn't swatting at his leg and running for the hose though, so maybe not.

The walk to Jeremy's took me away from the stilts a little further inland, to the paved parking lot of an isolated apartment building. Both the grass and the asphalt presented some kind of unavoidable bullshit. When circumstances forced me to choose between them, I scanned the gray sandy soil of the medians for the mounds that rose ominous like temples from the deep. Of course, to the fire ants *we* were the ruthless expansionists. Wherever they could make a stand, nations upon nations of the little zealots stood guarding their own slice of paradise against the titanic horrors all around them. Years of scars around my ankles bore testimony to that. I made it to Jeremy's apartment building and went up the elevator in silence.

When he opened the door, I smiled. I was thinking about the time he slammed it in my face. He wasn't the superficial sort, the beautiful saint, so it was hard to let him down. He was willing to be seen with me. He didn't judge me for being scruffy or a slob or for the general condition of my humanity. He did, however, refuse to share a place with me again until I could be happy on my own.

"So, how about that diagram?" I asked, slumping on a bean bag chair by a stack of beat literature.

"I tried. I really did. But I realized that there's no fucking way any of it is gonna come out right. The problem is that every medium I could use is too cumbersome, too simple. Words, images, it'd be like showing you a tin can and saying 'that's the starship I saw in the wheatfield last night.' Nothing compares and there are no words."

"Holy shit,"

"I'm telling you, you're gonna go there yourself someday. You are not ready... you're ready, but you're not ready, because nobody's ever ready."

"Someday then..."

"In the spirit of trying new things, I will *try* to explain..."

"Got anything to drink?"

"Uh, yeah. I got lime-aid, orange-aid, some passionfruit kombucha with a big ol' SCOBY, a big forest of green tea in the cupboard... Take your pick."

"I see," I said, disguising my disappointment that he had yet again disposed of his fine liquor in response to the light within.

"Okay..." he began, rubbing his hands together, "... It's like dying on a roller coaster and having an aeon open up the afternoon from inside your mind to show you the genetic inventory of the multiverse as it rests in an infinite space of potentials perpendicular to our own membrane." I sat back, eyebrows raised.

"Wow."

"It told me... The mantis told me that all information is a folding of space-time."

"A mantis?"

"Yes, Jedediah, the galactic mantis. Or the mantis of galaxies, all waltzing through each other and... or well, he's galaxies full of galaxies you see? All illuminated by the eyes of endless minds... I realized I was gazing into the interwoven lattice of their thoughts, my thoughts, the wordless mutual understanding of rabbits and pine trees laid bare...The inner kernels of both transcending the duality posed by each in their ipseity... Phrases of light unfurling in the deep. The audience... less a trial than a gem-laden affair... an affirmation of the love-absolute." His eyes drifted over to a rabbit scampering over the roots of an old tree and he smirked. His bedroom was decked out with framed images of natural parks, fractals, and arabesques. They each seemed to point to something in common that none of them could convey independently. I always admired his longing for the infinite life, breathing in and through every declension of form. He'd dress like a jester, he said, and travel from planet to planet in a flying outhouse, or a big hollowed-out trout with an olive branch in one hand and a stethoscope in the other. The warm summer air was tempered with a cool humid breeze from the sea. The scent of salt came to greet me through his open window. I could smell in that Atlantic air whiffs of his intoxicated dream.

"I don't know. It's not like anything I see or say can make the truth any more true."

"The way that can be walked is way too much," I said, quoting an old friend. Jeremy was silent. "Y'all right?" I asked.

"Yeah. Look what I got." Jeremy retrieved a Tupperware container full of pot pie.

"Oh shit..."

"Dad keeps telling me to bring you home for dinner. That is, when he'll be allowed to. He misses you."

"Is he that swamped?" I asked.

"The Apophatic Academy thinks he's alive for their convenience. They've got him selling books door to door!"

"I'd love to see him again. I'd have to take time to clean myself up first."

"Nah, you're fine. You're not that skeevy," said Jeremy, undoing the buckle of his leather belt. I chuckled.

"Barring any change in direction, how long do I have before I'm unspeakably crusty? Could he bear to be seen with me when I'm rotten through like driftwood?" I thought to myself. As Jeremy finished changing, he launched into a diatribe.

"I had this customer come up to me the other day talking at me nonstop for hours. It was surreal. After thirty minutes of nodding and hoping he would just leave I asked him a question, encouraging him. He'd maybe give a flicker of an acknowledgment and just blaze on in whatever direction he was going before. He talked about his favorite pet stores and who said what to who standing in line for groceries. I still don't know his name but I know his three cats' entire medical history from birth. Naturally, he didn't ask me anything about myself. Eventually I quietly and gently told him to fuck off."

"That's a little mean for you," I said.

"I think he was just lonely. I wasn't angry. It's just... What the hell was he expecting? Like I'm ever gonna be psyched playing the captive audience listening to drivel like that. That's not happening. That's not... ever happening. No wonder he was blathering to a total stranger. I was probably his last resort." Jeremy kneaded his brow and sighed. The calls of waves and gulls broke against our silence and turned back. The road went up a ways and gradually yielded to sand and standing water. Beyond was a street bathed in the sea. Porches and stilts bowed to the horizon, crowning mounds of rotting wood and the entrails of living rooms. Beach renewal failed ahead of schedule on Sassoon. The southern half of the island was gone.

2

Summer 'fifteen might well have been the beginning of time for the sainted haze smothering its memory. Fucked by its unforgettable excesses, the mosaic of our recollections had to be meticulously reconstructed over years through interminable debate like it was some lost apostolic age. Jeremy and I were caught up in an acid wave and were no more; those were the events as could be seen from the outside. When the beginningless and endless sea of nectar spat us out through into an evening on Eden's shores, we found the warp, weft, and whimper of fallen history somehow unbegun, born again.

It was the first and the seventh day. Arm in arm, fresh from the Heart, we tearfully accepted the gift of life that already beat within us. We strove to embalm ourselves in the same psychotropics that had, in our reckoning, lifted us from our sinking island home to something greater. We wanted to transform the transient bliss of a reckoning with the unspeakable into a talisman, a gem we could have flowing through our veins at all times, shielding ourselves from a rickety reality we had already forgotten was the Holy of Holies all along. Our egos, habits, and eccentricities grew stronger for every step taken in our victory march over them. The phenomenal con of the human game began to beguile us once more.

We became unrecognizable, partly on purpose. The days were a mirage of faces and farces. We entangled ourselves in stranger's lives until we were desperate to escape. Our jaunts left us strung along a complicated web of attachments. Our respective neurological safaris revolved around each other. We taught each other as we made case studies of ourselves. Deep within each of us was some rabid acolyte poised before a steep decline, ready to sacrifice the senses at the altar of love. Convinced of our invulnerability, we persisted until the burnout became too real to ignore. We learned that certain kinds of fun leave scars. With time we grew cold, even to each other.

It would have been wasted time, were it not the time of my life. That was when we could all still see each other, the summer. Soon after that summer our lives changed. Terry's uncle kicked him out. He took his gig money and joined up with an enclave of itinerant experimentalists out west. After spending most of the fall tending to said enclave's clandestine marijuana crop, he moved on to play actual music on the coast. His knowledge of the research chemical market made him a surprisingly auspicious recruit for a shoegaze duet called 'Gorg Is,' and later a synthpop quintet. His former legal guardian operating a pharmaceutical high-control group had sadly done far more for his networking ability than his miserable high-school career.

Like a sedated spectator at the back of an empty movie theater I watched the days flicker past in a bricolage film reel stitching one vignette into the next. The memories, blurry and indistinct, spilled seething into a great red tide of grain, fuzz, and foam. The corners of the frame were delineated by the brownish-brackish water of the river's beachhead into the sea. The columns and trusses sustaining the picture from within were woven from strangers' couches and the vine-choked trunks of trees. At the center is a bleary midnight walk to a taco truck. Sucked into the swirl of the same eternal moment, the eclectic assemblage lacked all past and future. Remembering the order of events added no depth to the textures churning onscreen. One conversation simply squeezed through the pauses and skips of another until the whole carnival turned to mush.

Sometimes all I would carry from an hours long conversation was a face or a name but hardly ever both. Their words and thoughts would echo again and again, sprouting from the fertile confusion as tangled threads of ideas whose roots and branches anchored my world in place. The fog of the bog of my mind deepened with every layer of tar I sucked into my lungs. I'm pretty sure that was just correlation. Looking back on that florid knot of footage carelessly spliced in post, I saw stillness in motion.

We ended up shouting into the sea most nights. It was the sea we loved most of all. The sun and all its dominions were senseless without it. Our scrapes winced in the cool plastic cling of artificial air. The shark tooth on Jeremy's necklace sat poised at his collarbone. We didn't realize then how free we were. We probably should have been afraid. All we wanted to do was go further and further. We hoped to inspect reality from the outside someday. We were hunting for an exit we already knew didn't quite exist.

"Come on Louie…" moaned Jeremy, clattering his phone down in disgust only to snatch it up again in a futile spiral.

"He's not coming."

"I'm texting Pete."

"Woah. No, you're not. Are you really going to put yourself through that shit again?"

"I'm buying bud. I don't care where I get it."

"But *Pete?* Maybe it's not worth three hours waiting in a parking lot."

"He's not *that* flaky. Besides, what do we know about his life?"

"All I'm saying is don't make any other plans for tonight.

You *know* this is gonna take a while."

There was a long silence.

"Do you ever worry that... that you'll just listen to anything?" he asked. I turned to him, sleepy eyed and said:

"What do you mean?"

"Like... What if what I like is shit?"

"Like you have shit taste?"

"Imagine you're enjoying dinner and you're the only one who doesn't know you're slopping shit out of a pail. What then? What if that's what my taste in music is like?"

"The fuck do you mean? You can't judge taste... It just is what it is. You know? You can't explain it. Words always fuck you over." We sat with the lull that followed, daydreaming of evenings past when we were flush. The dining room chandelier threw a little moonlight on our dim little den. Jeremy's parents had been out of town for a month or so and we'd made devilishly good use of the place as a salon for useless profundity. If we were more structure oriented as people then we'd probably have started some sort of organized religion. The need to say something pulled me back to the situation at hand.

"We could invite Terry to town and see what he's been up to. It's been months since we said we would call him. Maybe he's somewhere close to the state. And he could drive right back." I offered. Jeremy looked at me. I shrugged and looked away. Poor Terry. So, we sat around for another thirty minutes and hardly spoke a word to each other.

"I mean, he could be dead," suggested Jeremy, scrolling nervously.

"He's not dead."

"Are you sure about that? He didn't answer me last time."

"Well that doesn't mean he's dead," I said.

"I know."

"Maybe he just quit selling dope."

"He would never," said Jeremy.

"Well how's it any more likely that he's dead?"

"People die all the time. Besides, this guy makes too much money to quit."

"How much money could he be making? He sucks at this. He never *has* anything and when he *does,* he takes *five fucking hours* to show up in some shitty parking lot across the street from his house. His idea of a secure spot is a grocery store bathroom. I die whenever I have to go in there. We almost get caught *every fucking time,*" I said.

"He's got the wrong priorities for sure, he should be way more committed to selling drugs. Can you imagine a more dedicated base of customers?"

"So did he text back?" I sighed. I was getting a little weirded out by my relief at that sound of Jeremy's phone dinging.

"He's asking how much we want."

"I dunno, what do you want?" I asked. He paused for a moment.

"If I do fifty and you do fifty we could each get like… two grams I guess?"

"Sure," I said with glistening eyes. We waited around and briefly inspected his pipe for smokable resin. Finding none, we waited more and scrolled away our time.

"Has he said when he's free yet?" I asked.

"Last thing he said was 'k ilyk."

"Huh." I leaned back into my seat. And so, we waited until the sun dipped below the trees and the shallow din of cicadas seemed to slowly drift away into a sharp silence. Every moment was tedious, unnecessary.

"Okay, here we go," said Jeremy.

"What did he say?"

"Meet in thirty."

"Where?"

"He didn't say," so Jeremy asked him. It took thirty minutes for him to respond.

"He says 'Bingo's at nine.'"

"So... another hour?" I said, enunciating every word with a tension that was singular and pure. He shrugged my frustration off.

"It'll come when it'll come. We can be happy without it."

"I know. So why go to the trouble?" We sat. Finally, when the sky was pitch dark, we decided to stand and stumble on. We were silent as we wound down the road. The trees crowded in on us with their silent feelers. Small roads at night felt like a shooting gallery. Our route became narrower and narrower. Soon we were winding by screaming tons of metal mere degrees from mutual annihilation. Night after night I'd wake up in bed after driving the wrong way down a five-lane highway, crashing into a ditch or getting pulled over for reckless weaving. Sometimes the nightmare would involve leaving the car and forgetting to take it off drive, and being crushed between it and a dumpster. Not realizing that these were dreams, I would reel in terror and sit up blinking in the early hours of the morning. We bantered about the mysteries of the day. The grocery store was in another jurisdiction, some garden of earthly delights called 'Surfer's Point' by a mainland beach we'd never been to. I squinted at my brick as Jeremy messed with the MP3 player at a stoplight.

"Okay, there's some big golf course over there, somewhere..." He and I looked around. We saw the cops pull over some guy in a Mustang who rode our asses in a delirious rage for a hot minute and flew past us through a red light into the rain. From that second on Jeremy focused on nothing but the road. At first, we thought the police were coming for us, nailing us in the act of scurrying around town for ditch weed.

"I don't really know where the Bingo's is."

"Isn't there one out in Aubourg?"

"No man that's the Meal Mink."

"Fuck me, I don't remember either."

"Well he just texted 'leaving soon' so we better find this place."

"Gimme that. I'll figure it out," I said. He handed me his phone. "You know, it freaks me out that you're still texting and driving after what happened."

"I've forgiven myself for it," he said, and typed in 'Bingo's.' He opted for the closest of the two. We pulled into the lot and found it even sparser than expected. We were nearly the only people there, minus a white van and a station wagon. "Man, what if someone comes around and asks why we're sitting here doing *nothing?*" he asked, getting edgy.

"You're being paranoid," I said.

"Am I? I've been ambushed in the woods. They could reliably bag fifteen dope-horny geeks in those woods a weekend if word somehow never got around. Peaceful herbivores, minding their *own* fucking business and *BAM*." His chapped lips bore marks of inner tension.

"They did? They *did*, that's right."

"Yeah. I went waaaay out there in the quiet dark and they *still* found me. I was with a few friends, so maybe we were easier to catch. This one kid, this pledge was talking loud about how much he loved his brothers-to-be for force feeding him coke and bourbon and dumping the frat once the hazing got bad. The police must have figured out the kids on south campus were using the woods as an ashtray a long time ago and now they just merrily go in there to pluck people out at night. Could been a lot worse."

"That was last October, right? You were hysterical. You

thought the school was going to throw you out," I remembered.

"*God,* imagine if they'd caught us tripping sack out there."

"*Fuck* that."

"Ah, and here he is. He just said 'omw.'"

"Nice, about time, it's almost 9:30."

"It's gonna be worth it."

"Do you think we'll still be smoking weed and dropping acid in four years?"

"Nah, like why? We'll have graduated by then. I'm sure by then we'll be so busy we won't have the desire to smoke anymore. Everyone cuts back eventually."

"Yeah," I murmured.

"And I'm basically done taking acid already. I've pretty much won against my ego. I walk around and I don't see my ego and I don't hear my ego and I can't sense my ego because, clearly, I killed it and deserve special recognition for my accomplishment," he said, puffing out his chest. Sometimes he embodied his mock-ups so sincerely I worried that the imperceptible boundary between satire and real, sincere inflation had been crossed. If I could be convinced, I was Jedediah Greer, I could be convinced of anything. A sufficiently enjoyable act is liable to sweep anyone off their feet, just as a sufficiently unpleasant reality invites denial.

Layers of personality clothe raw oceanic consciousness as a mercy to all. As the brain branched its way to self-reflection, it began to suffocate under the barnacle deposits of its own inherited architecture. They help the mind multiply its many selves, but they are certainly not purpose-driven to work for the benefit of the individual entity ironically endowed with the most complex instrument in the cosmos of its own understanding. Once it learned how to invent problems, it began reinventing the world, not necessarily for its own benefit either. I still believe all it wants is to be left to its own wonderful silence, to be rid of all it has come to embody while seeming only to be asleep.

"You've really done well for yourself there," I said. "When's he gonna get here?"

"How far is he?"

"Prolly like thirty minutes, right?"

"Yeah. Wait, actually no," I said, stopping to think. Jeremy looked at me, waiting for me to remember.

"Oh, yeah, there was that."

"Yeah, his ex-roommate is still on the run. I don't think that place is inhabited, like, at all anymore. I think he lives in Terry's old house now. You know the one his uncle almost burned down? How far away is that?" I asked.

"That's definitely over the bridge. Could be forty-five minutes, an hour even." forty minutes went by.

"He says he's here," said Jeremy. "Where the fuck is *here*?" We looked around. We were alone. The Bingo's was still open.

"Well he must be lying," I said. "Oh shit. We're in the wrong lot."

"Amazing. How long until we can get to the other one?" asked Jeremy. I set a course.

"twenty minutes." He telegraphed the bad news as he fired up the engine and pulled out of the lot. Jeremy stopped at a red light and read the brick in his lap. He shook his head.

"I can't believe this."

"What?"

"He's going home. He says he forgot the stuff."

"No way, no *fucking* way," I moaned as another siren split the evening air. We finally pulled into the other Bingo's at around 10:45. We waited another forty minutes. My compatriot was getting impatient, texting every ten minutes for updates. "Let's just go home and put our feet up, forget about all this shit," I suggested. He slowly turned to look at me, shook his head very slowly, and looked back at his phone into the quest.

Pete pulled up at around midnight. He nodded at us through his windshield as he turned off his engine. He was equal parts untrimmed and tidy with his apostolic beard and kind, sensible eyes closed off by some impenetrable distance. Jeremy volunteered to have me go in and meet him. My legs felt like twigs bound by straw. I didn't even look in Pete's direction as we entered from opposite ends of the store. I stopped to examine some boxes of cereal. I quietly read the labels off soup cans, just in case the cameras had microphones as well. To my right I heard Pete shutting the bathroom door all the way at the back of the store. I imagined someone in a little box somewhere examining my mannerisms for ill intent and dared not look. I really took my sweet time getting there, horrified at the apparatus in my mind. When I opened the door Pete was nowhere to be found. I decided to wash my hands so as not to look like an anxious bride alone at the altar. I heard the toilet flush and realized he was in the stall. He joined me at the sink to my left. He looked to his right as he turned the hot water valve and said, "Sup."

"Hey man. What's up?"

"Not much man, what about you?"

"Not bad, not bad, I appreciate." We had both reached into our pockets when the bathroom door opened and a man with a bitter, worn store uniform hanging from his frame slid into the doorway, staring. He turned and walked away, his eye fixed on us. I could have dropped my body and sailed through the stars right there and then. I was shaken to the depths. Pete pulled out a crumpled sheet of paper with a calm sort of urgency and put it in my outstretched hand as I mashed hundred bucks into his. We walked swiftly, but not too swiftly, out of the store. We couldn't see the guy, but that didn't guarantee he couldn't see us. Pete played it a little cooler than I did, making small talk about a fishing trip. When we got outside, we just nodded to each other and went our separate ways. I couldn't decide whether to walk or jog to Jeremy's humming car.

"Drive," was all I said when I shut the door. We made our way back cautiously and lit up as discreetly as possible in his parent's backyard around a wooden table. We were soon carried aloft by peals of laughter when we realized that the paper, he handed me was his calculus homework. I remember learning later on that he was a pretty swell guy, punctual outside of his side gig, and like me had trouble integrating logarithms.

We were having conversations that would echo through our lives for years. We knew even then how much we would miss that summer. Our worries slipped between the cracks splitting the known world asunder. We could be free and together only if we could ride the waves, find balance in the storm. For once in our rational, serious, certain lives we had some understanding of the need to recognize our own ignorance. I think by 1 a.m. or so everything was on some kind of time delay, the current moment was obscured by the foggy afterimage of the preceding two seconds.

"Can you imagine what science is going to do to this plant when it's taken off Schedule?" I asked Jeremy.

"That'd be something. I mean, in some parts of this country that's already underway. Imagine what a few *hundred* years of tinkering will do. Stuff's already powerful. If it gets any stronger, I wonder if I'll be able to handle myself. Like, imagine you work up to 1,000 milligrams a day in some nightmare habit made possible by science. If you can't overdose, what will all that extra THC do to your routine? Either the high feels the same after a while and it's just this depressing case study of the hedonic treadmill, or the experience is fundamentally different in which case we've taken something relatively innocuous and made it more debilitating."

"1000 miligrams? There's always someone out there who scoffs at that. Why not 5,000? Why not 10?"

"Oh shit. Helpless brains."

"Like leaves adrift in the blue deep."

"That'd almost be hilarious if it wasn't," I said, leaning back and listening to the walls breathe around me. I knew then: If you can't shake the feeling you're wasting your life, you almost certainly are. I was free and in love. For once I knew exactly who, what, and where I was supposed to be.

3

June 2019. I rounded a corner and the sun in all its glory stared me down. Through my fingers I saw a sunburnt chin through a thin goatee bathing in the beer dribbling from a styrofoam cup. As I focused in, a doe nuzzled up at the side of the mighty guzzler.

"What a lucky man, to have drawn all God's creatures to his little shindig!" I thought. On second glance, the doe became a crumpled lawn chair digging into his thigh. The cup rolled onto an ant's nest as the man fell into blissful sleep. The doe had been as real to me as the daylight. To catch the trickster's hoax at work at the frayed edges of perception, one need only have eyes or ears or thoughts at the very least. The mind imbues shadows with form and shape just as they come into view, complete with an assigned role in the scheme of things. Anything can vanish just like the doe, with no history left behind and no future left unattained. All it takes is recognizing it wasn't there in the first place. Shadows may still come to play, but for the game to once again be convincing it must somehow be forgotten again. Only then can anything come into being. Arriving at the busiest part of town and realizing I had no games to play, I turned back.

Returning to a pigsty, my brain beat me with a hail of accusations of senseless ingratitude. My ashtray looked like a volcanic desert spilling over its rims to coat the glossy grain of my desk. I couldn't remember the last time I'd emptied the thing. I would have then and there, but my ability to notice problems far exceeded my will to solve them. My buzz from the morning had simmered down. My train of thought went from a blast front of warm, colorful fascination into a rusty, joyless carousel ride swinging hither and yon like a broken chandelier. Hours before I was the happy child in a tidal pool. Now I was at the bottom of a well. I only ever wore the Sock or the Buskin in those days, without desiring to do so or feeling a need to explain why.

Once saturated in superabundance, the room around me pulsated with a drowned out, menacing vibe. The face of the world that stared back into me was weary and worn. Cadaverous lips and gums slid away, baring the jester's fangs. I checked for a pulse. When was death coming for me? In a month? A year? I could feel the scythe poised at my neck. I was a skiff of ice sliding through an offshore typhoon. Little devils leveled their bony fingers at me smiling out of the corners of their eyes.

I uttered a pious phrase and smoked another bowl. Acrid tar built its smoldering nation in my chest. Smoking in ages past, I used to be able to pour a cup of coffee and take thirty minutes to remember to drink it for sheer delight in everything else. My senses would just fan out and frolic. Now I was always retreating inward, away from life in all its variety. What happened to delighting in the little things, the grandest of all? When did other people, their beautiful faces, and their wonderful smiles become like so many road signs and barriers on the path back to splendid isolation? I felt my muscles strain around my skull. My thoughts meandered, muddled and confused like ants on a plastic feast. Was I sinking out of touch with the world at large? Or had the world drifted apart too slowly to see? And so, the days went by like static.

I opted for distraction. I hazily scrolled through a column of thumbnails never intended to be remembered. It did not horrify me then how many terabytes of horseshit I force fed myself on a daily basis without desiring to do so or feeling a need to explain why. Then I saw a ghost and my heart stopped. The image on the video was my ex and I. That was exactly what I was afraid of. I couldn't help but laugh at the idea of the two of us making videos for the internet. We'd uploaded it on a harm reduction kick. The clean-shaven young buck I saw on-screen hadn't been seen in public for years. I assumed Eve hadn't altered course too much. She had a keen sense for that kind of thing. I clicked to a moment right before the end of the video. We were sitting in some arboretum discussing our experiences with psychedelics and how not to royally fuck yourself in the course of taking them.

"The best part, for me, has got to be the afterglow. Your experience is fresh in your mind. It's like you're riding into… everything you just left. And that's the best news ever. You're still up enough to be absolutely engrossed with life while not being too shaken up to go outside," she said. Then I responded:

"It's a more useful time for sure. You know, personally I think that by the time you're coming down you're getting more and more entangled in solid concepts. You exchange the heightened intuition for a more grounded perspective. You're more constructive on the comedown because you're closer to your everyday self. It's easier to drive a car, but it's also easier to get road rage."

"Well we're always prone to getting angry, the question is do we remember what it costs?" Eve took a water bottle from her bag as I rambled on,

"What I like is coming across a door, with a friendly voice on the other end asking me to come in. I close my eyes, lean back, and I'm home. And that's the end of me, that's the end of everything, because I'm home again. Those moments sustain me."

Eve took that as the cue for her end-the-video monologue. I

stuffed my flashcards into my shirt-pocket more fastidiously than I ever would off camera. "Now, the most important thing for you to remember is that psychedelics can be very harmful whether you use or misuse them. First, make sure that what you have is really what you think it is. Find a testing kit to identify what you're looking for and don't risk your life to do something you don't need to do. 25i-NBOME or any number of research chemicals have been sold as LSD, an objectively safer chemical, and killed people. Remember what folks say: if it's bitter, it's a spitter."

"There are psychological risks too, even with the real deal. Whatever you try to bury will confront you. For some people predisposed to certain kinds of mental illness, psychedelics, can accelerate their manifestation. Even if you have the kind of brain that can respond in a healthy manner to the psychedelic experience and can get something out of it, if you aren't careful about what environment or state of mind you take it in you can come away with lasting trauma, changes in personality... So please, everyone..."

"*DO YOUR FUCKING RESEARCH!*"

I smiled. Those two wide-eyed kids dressed up in snappy coats and quips were like the sight of a remote shore to a drowning man, eliciting grief when forever out of reach. Since the breakup and graduation and everything I'd buried my memories of her. Over years I lost or threw away everything that harbored her image. It wasn't intentional. Ironic, that in an epoch when our public selves are best preserved the mementos of our sad dead ends are as eager as ever to be jostled into the underworld of lost phrases and photographs.

Those memories resurfaced unceasingly as new nightmares. To enter the ocean of bliss, one must cross over their seas of human baggage. That kind of crossing would undo me. I could almost hear the pummeling lecture I'd be given by this or that aeon, higher self, or clear and cogent thought before the seamless transition into current affairs. They would all indicate the trash bags overflowing with bottles, the carpet dotted with tar, the heart filled with misdirected derision and self-imposed alienation. I would have to confront the unsustainability of my whole mess.

The brain is always groping for balance. Should a catastrophe turn the world upside-down, the new arrives only to dull, and stasis reasserts itself. Most ordinary sensations are overpowering at first. This must be how we got bored with our unimaginable situation. Our billiard sailing through space and time is full of interlocking, self-transforming, self-replicating intelligences. We woke up one day and it was all ho-hum. Psychedelics may offer the world as splendid as the seventh day or so horrendous that we would rather have it barren and void. Life itself is the greatest surprise, numinous, full of terror, full of beauty, cruel, kind, and inescapable.

The suffering of others becomes impossible to ignore. At a sufficiently high dosage, one can believe another's suffering to be one's own. Seeing all things made equal in their unity, the panoply of nature suggests that which is one and unseen. Concern for self and other merges into a love that transcends all distinction. The eons of struggle for survival bleed through our every instinct. Is there anyone deserving of forgiveness in a world so ravaged by the consequences of love and cherishing? When we have disowned one another? Yet our need to forgive outshines all. All compulsion is undone.

"Come home. Let go," it would ask. If I ever picked up the phone again, I feared sinking into a hell I couldn't even fathom in my dreams. How do you return to paradise if you've lost it? I felt the sting of garden tar in my lungs.

I went to the fridge. Amid the rotting vegetables and half

empty containers of parmesan cheese I spotted something promising. I pulled the bottle out for further inspection: vermouth. I didn't have a clue how it came to me. Maybe Terry left it? I opened it up and took a whiff. It didn't smell right. Then again, I didn't know what 'right' was supposed to smell like. I cringed a little, weighing it in my hand ponderously. I knew I was going to drink the whole thing. I looked back at my little box of blue light and wondered whether she'd tried to forget me as hard as I was trying to forget her. I wondered whether she drew solace or remorse from what remained of our long-abandoned work. We'd promised each other that even if we broke up, we'd never give up on who we were to each other. I upturned the bottle, a stranger and a hypocrite.

I woke up with someone kicking me in the side. Absolutely no-one was there. My entire body was sore; I didn't know why. The sight of the blue sky stifled the curse rising from my throat; the cold deep stared into me. The waters lapped on the shore all wild and dark and tinged with green and brown. I darted to my feet. The joint hanging from my mouth toppled onto the sand. A crab swooped by and grabbed it, darting back to its lair faster than thought. Maybe it was just my imagination telling me to run before twin abysses claimed my body for unknowable purposes. I shivered violently under the rising sun and whistled through chattering teeth. I bade the abyss of above and below good day.

***

Terry said he was coming to visit. That is in fact what he said. He didn't tell me that he'd have Eve under his arm when he came to the door. I pranced up to the door with a spliff and a brew and pulled the creaking door back. I felt the skin on the back of my neck burn and my stomach drop into my feet. I lost all sense of balance and stood there looking at the two of them from three feet over my head.

"We don't have to sleep in your bed... We can sleep on the floor, or the couch or something. We're not picky."

"How did you think this was going to go?" Was this a misguided attempt to bridge an old gap? Or was it just carelessness?

"Terry knew you'd let him sleep on your couch, but I thought if you knew *I* was coming too you'd say no..."

"Last I heard, *you* certainly have the disposable income to put yourselves up somewhere."

"I *can* go somewhere else if you're not cool with this. It's just... I can't talk to you on the phone anymore so." Her hair was generally the same sort of blonde as before but more subdued somehow. "I'm sorry I didn't tell you we were together. But we're here now and we could really use a friend."

"I just struggle with understanding how you would feel if I showed up on your doorstep after not talking to you for a year? With Terry? Who could have *said something.*"

"Look, our apartment's gonna be ready soon. We'd be out of your hair... soon-ish. I understand if you don't want to help us but..." she trailed off, looking hurt and looking for words "...I'd be surprised. After everything we went through together..."

"Everything we *put* each other through. Look, I love you both. You've been there for me and..." I cringed "...I'll always be there for you too. But not tonight. Ask before jumping for closure like this." In retrospect, I did feel like a dick. These were people I cared about. I didn't object to love. I felt stabbed in the back anyway. It was the lie by omission that stung and confused me. Did they trust me or didn't they?

"I didn't know you were still this broken up over the breakup, I just thought I'm sorry, Jed. It really was my idea. I thought you'd be happier to see us."

"I'm happy to see you two... It's the *way* I'm finding out about things here. Y'all see that, right? That *this* is a bit of a surprise?"

"It's okay. We'll just find somewhere else," she said as her tone plummeted. Terry had gotten gaunt since he left for the west. He'd lined his arms with tattoos and let his reddish-brown hair grow out. I leaned on the doorframe looking down at my shoes and tried to say something like I'm sorry about how I'm taking this. I turned to go inside as they turned to leave, but left the door open until they pulled out of the driveway.

"You don't have to be such a stranger, you know? None of us are out to get you," said Eve before shutting the passenger door. I looked up at all the dreams I had with her as the gravel whinged under his wheels. I remember when they could no longer bear me up. I felt relieved. I stopped wasting effort on a life that was killing me slowly. I retreated into a life that I assumed was possible, sane, and secure. Sinking deep into the easy chair once belonging to my uncle and his whippet Arnold was, after all, the path of least resistance.

I once asked Eve what was more important in life, liberty or security. She was working for a bank at the time and she said security. I asked Terry the same question when he was wandering on the road and he said liberty. My abode offered both, a rare security, a peculiar liberty, demanding only that I surrender aspirations beyond the sinking island of Sassoon. Should I embrace the security of liberty or the liberty of security on more stable ground, I would forfeit both.

***

That night, I dreamt that my mother was still alive. She'd been whisked away to a far country. I wasn't allowed to see her, nor to have any contact with her by order of the king's jester, lest I somehow disturb the balance of the world.

I woke up and went out onto the porch. It felt narrower than usual. The sky was wider. From the gray came a raindrop that snuck into my eye and dribbled down the side of my nose. I remembered when my mother would sing 'You Are My Sunshine' to wake me up as a very small child. I could still see her face. I'm sure there were days when I would smile and drape my arms over her shoulders, squeezing. But I could only remember the days when I turned away, groaning. I desperately wished I could show her gratitude. My every mistake and shortcoming welled up out of the morning silence. Did she know that I loved her? Did she know there was more to her progeny than a selfish grub? Maybe there wasn't. I rolled a joint and strove to forget.

4

He felt algae swelling up in his lungs. The bodies of his friends hung motionless, skewered by rays of sunlight. Their silhouettes slid into a shower of crabs, fish, and squid. Finally, the blinding sun broke through the torrent in a geyser of foam. Jeremy gasped as his breath returned. His hand went to his throat. He couldn't explain these spells of suffocation. He went for his phone and the music that always brought him back to his senses, back to his life. With Jobim accompanying on guitar, Jeremy labored over an omelet beneath the golden light of dawn, glancing over at the great disc rising up over Sasson's tiled skyline. The sight of it left imprints which simmered over his morning tasks like burns on a film. He cracked an egg over a pan of sizzling garlic and felt his chest swell with every pluck and pull of the strings.

He rounded a corner and sat down on a pillow and ate his breakfast on the wooden dining room floor, which also counted as his living room. The comforting music was muffled. A faux marble bust moaned at him for a bite from the other end of the room. Another statuette on the far corner laughed at the bust's frozen agony. The cackling of seagulls came in clean and crisp from the street as they had their primeval conniptions over garbage. He looked over at his phone lying on the floor. He let the impulse to grab it pass.

As he was washing his dishes, he glanced out the window and saw Terry and Eve coming up the sidewalk. They were five feet apart. Terry was trailing off with the gulls. He'd catch up with her, then his gaze would drift back to the birds still screaming for trash. Jeremy walked onto the balcony and waved. They waved back. Everyone was wearing pastel colors as if to complement the edifices around them.

"Don't tell me…" said Jeremy.

"We live here now!" answered Eve. They disappeared into the building and re-appeared at his door.

"They only just gave us the keys. We were living in an icebox earlier," said Terry.

"An expensive icebox," she added. Jeremy followed them out the door and down the hall. The entire apartment was empty, except for a few boxes lying around.

"I'd just as soon stay in Asheville than sleep in that inn down the street. Weren't your parents willing to take you in for a bit?"

"Maybe, I don't know. I think if I went back there to live, they'd just start holding their roof over my head again, making my decisions for me. I really don't need that," she sighed.

"It might have been nice. We haven't even had the space to move Eve's furniture out east. We've got the key and a few odds and ends, that's all."

"Still got your book collection Terry?" asked Jeremy, trying to make conversation.

"I was able to keep some of them for a while. My brother claims I ran off with a lot of his, but that's only because they were gifts to both of us. I'm the one who actually read them… Then I had to sell them all for a month's rent."

"The band broke up?" Terry nodded.

"The lead singer married the lead bassists'… was it his aunt?" asked Eve.

"No, no, see the lead singer was *going* to marry the bassist's mom. The bassist though, he didn't find out until like a week before it was supposed to happen. All I know is she picks up the lead singer up at an afterparty and we hardly saw him after that. We didn't know why. We were struggling to even come up with a consistent sound. I mean, we were fucked. It turns out he was sipping white wine at art galleries that whole time. If he showed up to record something he hardly said two words to anyone. He practically slept through the production of an album he'd been planning for years. After a month of this shit she breaks it off with him a week before the wedding. She got on a plane to Cologne, and that was it…" Terry trailed off.

"That's what happens when you think of art as a way to buy people's admiration, once you get it all the effort stops, you backslide without even realizing it," said Eve.

"Yeah, it's not really attractive to give up on your calling the moment you get comfortable. At this point he was basically out of the band. He showed up all snotty and sniveling holding up the little paragraph she sent. That was the first time he explained any of this shit."

"Damn… The bassist must've been pissed. Did he accept the singer's apology?" asked Jeremy.

"The singer didn't apologize. He just gave up and skipped town with all our recordings. That was the final straw for the rest of the band, which was the shittiest thing of all. Last I heard he was living in some intentional community as far off the grid as you can go."

"Fuck me, that's… *Fuck*," said Jeremy.

"Yeah, so that's kind of why I don't have any of my stuff here… or anywhere else really. Of course, that's not *really* what landed me on my ass, but you can see how it set the scene for what happened," said Terry. Jeremy nodded slowly, threading his hands through his curly brown hair.

"Well, I'm glad you two are back," he said. Eve smiled and picked up her guitar from a corner and began to strum.

"So, Terry and I are taking a crack at it, just us two. We're trying to think of names."

"For...?"

"Our band! Our thing!" answered Eve.

"Oh, right, yeah," said Jeremy, sniffing the air. "So, uh, you two are back together?"

"We are. Not that we were expecting to be, he needed help and I had a place to stay. I never thought for a *million* years that I was still in love with him, but when he showed up at my door, we were right back in the woods together looking at the moon. I can't explain it," said Eve. "We played a little music together, you know. I wasn't very confident since I put the guitar down but we were really into what we were making. It inspired me to give music another try."

"Likewise," said Terry, lacing his fingers with hers.

"And you're all moved in together?"

"We both wanted to come home, even though it felt like admitting failure. Even if nobody here wanted to see us again, we would at least be alone together in a place we both knew."

"You should have showed up at Gabriela's. She's got this amazing setup in her basement and everything..." said Jeremy.

"Are you seeing anyone right now?" asked Eve. Jeremy leaned back, looking at the ceiling.

"Not since Greg ran off to save the rainforest. I'm mostly focused on work and being a good dad to my succulents."

"And smoking with Jed," said Terry.

"Well, it keeps him from boozing all the time. He's not a very social drinker. He doesn't like to be around people when he cuts loose."

"That's him all right," sighed Eve.

"The more I pester him, the healthier he is."

"Does he hate us?" asked Terry.

"No. I think he hates himself or thinks he ought to. But no, he respects you two. He didn't really understand y'all showing up uninvited in the dead of night after years of silence but... he just needs time," answered Jeremy. He looked around.

"Y'all got anything to smoke?"

"Yes, we do," chirped Terry, springing to his feet.

"It is *8 a.m.* my dude," said Eve.

"I mean, I don't have work today," said Jeremy.

"I do and so do you, bucko," she said to Terry.

"...I quit that job." Eve's smile vanished. Terry inhaled, exhaled, and announced: "Eve, I fucking hate bagging groceries."

"Oh, and I don't? I'm sticking to the plan *we* agreed to. Happiness all the time forever was not a part of the deal."

"You should come and work with me. Gabby and I basically run the convenience store 'cause the boss is always on Clydesboro island doing taxidermy with..." said Jeremy, cutting himself short.

"...Fuck," said Terry, going to his stash under the bed.

"Terry, when were you going to tell me you quit your job?" asked Eve, angrier than she looked.

"When it came up. I'm a free and independent human being," he protested.

"We are in this *together*. You have to tell me these kinds of things!" she replied.

"Look, all right, yesterday a customer yelled at me so I yelled back. Customer's always right so I got shitcanned, even though they started it. It's embarrassing and I didn't want to say anything."

"So, you didn't even think I'd never mind. It's fine. It's fine. I think I need to take a walk before work. It's been nice catching up Jeremy. Don't be a stranger."

"Be kind; help people!" he replied as she slammed the door behind her. Jeremy turned to Terry.

"Terrence, what do you think of jumping down the rabbit hole again, like old times?"

"Old times? My bandmates and I tripped all the time. Wouldn't be anything out of the ordinary for me." Terry smiled as he answered. He didn't want to show it too much, but he reveled in something, anything familiar.

"Good. Now we just have to get Jed into the idea."

"He doesn't trip so well."

"That's because he's ashamed of himself."

"We're all finding our way. Didn't he swear it off?"

"Yeah but I know him. He's still curious, talks about it all the time. He's just scared as hell. His wits are telling him to hang on or he'll lose them."

"I don't know where you're gonna source your stuff. I don't have shit for connections up here. I've got some phenethylamine analogs but I know they scare you shitless."

"LSD was a research chemical once. The only ones I'm against are the ones with an LD50 smaller than a grain of dust." There was a moment of silence.

"Why do you want him to trip so bad?"

"It's not like I'll die if he doesn't. I guess a part of me misses when we were all younger. We'd trip sack together. We'd learn together. We'd heal together. I figure if he heals, he'd want to do more than just drink," said Jeremy.

"Yeah but… Don't the two of you get wasted together?"

"Guilty. That's not exactly helping. But this *might*. And it'd be *fun.*"

"It *might* be fun, Jer-bear. It might be like getting keelhauled through a meat grinder for him. That's how things went last time."

"Maybe that's where the healing comes in. *Something* has to show him the impact that abandoning hope has had on his body, his mind, his…"

"I mean… he *is* looking like shit these days. I always thought he'd pity me if I showed up on his doorstep. But now I pity him."

"That's why we've gotta offer help. Know what? I'm gonna go check on him. Nice seeing you Terry!"

"You too…"

***

The light breaking through the clouds was a subdued yellow. Jeremy and I were idling outside of a sparsely marked one story building in a rundown commercial district full of one-story buildings.

"It *is* messed up, Jed. It just doesn't sound like they were thinking all that much. I mean, it's been a good two years since they left home, they could've lost some common sense along the way. If they were trying to hurt you, I don't think they'd be apologizing every twenty minutes like they have for the past week," he said as my phone vibrated. "Ever gonna talk to them again? I will say, it's hard to give enough of a shit to apologize even once these days. They're our friends. It means something that they still give a shit." I paused at his question.

"Yes."

"It's hard, but giving people the benefit of the doubt pays off, sometimes. I will say this though: they didn't say *jack shit* about this whirlwind romance of theirs before coming to town," said Jeremy. He was trying to wipe a shard of shatter off on the coils of his vape rig. He screwed the cap on and took a deep pull. By the time his car was full of clouds and retching coughs I had my answer.

"I just don't wanna be negative. Like, why ostracize our friends over a stupid mistake? I haven't spoken to her or about her since that St. Patty's day parade; I have a heart attack when I see her picture anywhere. Anyone could have assumed I was way past it by now... Which I definitely am."

"Right."

"I dunno. Maybe they thought I'd just be so happy to see them that I wouldn't mind a surprise. He'd stride up to the door and say 'hey old buddy, look, it's our long-lost pal!' and things would be like they were in high school."

"I wanna believe that, y'know? Eve's a gem and so is Terry. But he was there when you two splits. He had to have known you were crushed over her. I guess if someone pulled something like that on me, I'd feel betrayed even if it was just an honest fuck-up," he said, handing me the rig. I pulled hard and died coughing.

"I get where you're coming from. It's cool and all to have them back, but why she'd wanna leave Asheville is beyond me. She was making bank over there."

"I guess being sad in Asheville is possible. What's really sad is we don't know why," said Jeremy. I nodded silently but had nothing more to add. We got out of his car and walked down a side stair to Kasino's front door. It was a different kind of spot, a former auto shop transformed into an offbeat community center. Their beverages were intended to lubricate conversation without reducing the drinker to incoherence. The menu, in neon glory, offered a cornucopia of herbal cocktails and a smattering of synthetic highs ranging from the saccharine to the nauseating, grown in greenhouses where possible so as not to further plunder nature's blessed coffers. I asked for a drink and went to find a seat.

I sat with my brimming mug of shouting, raving tea and burned my lips on its edge. Jeremy sauntered to my side with a root smoothie. We sat on a fence by a birdbath on a marble picnic table in the open air.

"I got something that might help you out of your slump," Jeremy said.

"Oh?" I raised an eyebrow, sipped, and gagged.

"I got two tickets to these feckless fuckwits called the Crumpled Bumpkins and about eight grams of…" he looked behind him, "…*psilocybe cubensis in my pocket.*"

"Eight?" I whispered.

"I know, right? Scary. Not commanding you to get back in the saddle or anything. That last trip *was* a bit of a… fuck. Still, the phone's here whenever you wanna give it a ring. Show starts in an hour, wanna go?" I huffed. I looked around wondering if anyone had heard us. Then my face became silent and still, worried my environment might scrutinize me back. Jeremy smiled at me, almost cracking up at my paranoia.

"Everything's going to be fine. Whatever happens, passes," he said.

"Let's go see… Who were these people again?" So, we piled into his tiny yellow car and sped away.

***

Jeremy was unscrewing the cap of his vape rig before he parked. He scraped a fat dab onto the coils. It looked like a glob of tar, rough stuff. Reaffixing the cap, he offered me his little box and I sucked on it. My lungs stung like they were being ripped open with pliers.

"Shit, that was a little too big. Sorry Pal," he said as I dry heaved over the glove box. Nature crinkled into focus. The textures of leaves began to drift and sprouted subtle, shimmering veins of color. I handed the rig back to him and covered my eyes and bent over, hacking into my own lap.

"All right, you ready?" he asked, dairy wisps of vapor billowing from his mouth.

"Yeah, just a sec," I managed to wheeze through the pain. We entered an ocean of light. I was about to fade away in that crowded colosseum. You could read it on my face. Lights flashed like technicolor bolts from the blue, entrancing throngs of the young and old alike. The walls teemed with electric sheep, creeping fractals, and pocket dimensions emanating from projectors spinning in air. Only when some of the smoke had cleared could I see the two bumpkins through the racket. They were dressed as strawmen with big smiles smeared over their masks with black paint. They looked dead. One sat at a keyboard with synthesizers and boxes galore. The other was looping spacy shit on a stool with a guitar, thrumming only the deepest notes.

My internal monologue shrank back, aghast at everything. Then a wall of noise split the ceiling open. It was an endless reverb of blended radio dramas from the end of a millennium that never was. Beneath it all I could distinguish a faint and familiar piano melody. They called their opus Universe Reset. It seemed to pass in fifteen minutes, but in truth it lasted an hour. We proceeded to have a gestural conversation with the bartender and sipped on some eight-dollar hint-of-beer seltzer. Somehow, I felt like I had a one-up on Terry, whose innocent and ferocious love of bizarre music always reflected a spark of something we aspired to. Had he seen the Crumpled Bumpkins, the exciting new duo out of Sassoon? When we left the venue I said, "That was an *amazing* fucking song. Can you imagine what the album's gonna be like?"

"I think that *was* the album. Like one long log of shit," said Jeremy. By the time we got back to my place we were both crossfaded and a touch disappointed. He rolled the window down as I shut the passenger's side door, turning to face him.

"Are you still... good to drive?" I had to ask him.

"I think I am but the cops might disagree. Wish I had a breathalyzer."

"Well, try not to get a DUI... or worse."

"Oh, absolutely brilliant suggestion my friend. I feel this powerful wisdom just radiating off you tonight. It's uncanny. Well done. Oh, and Jed?" I turned again. "Be good to yourself and others."

***

The next morning, I woke up feeling wrung out and rotten like an eggshell washed up in the muck of a polluted river, covered in brine flies. My mind balked at the sight of my own home. The faint intonations of conversations happening outside were like whining mosquitoes nipping at my ears. With what energy I had, I slumped back onto the couch. Rummaging, I found a bottle of wine I'd stuffed between the cushions the day before. I pulled the cork out with my teeth and spat it across the room.

"Whatever happens, happens," I said and upended it into my gullet till all sensation soured. I turned on my big screen and let recreations of war, weariness and the agonies of history trundle on as if they could soothe my soul. Whatever relief I found drinking I paid back with interest. I imagined some big cudgel taking wedges out of my liver, feeding them into the great yawning maw of addiction. The deeper in debt to the drink I went the less I realized that I was drinking to escape the wasteland of its own creation. Was binge drinking a part of my culture, or a corrosive thief of human excellence and wisdom? Can a drug become less dangerous if it's integrated into the rituals of society in some meaningful and sustainable way? Is that possible with a substance like ethanol? What purpose could it possibly serve? Any positive side to drinking is exactly as ephemeral as the buzz, which vanishes all too soon with our vitality. I looked up at the screen and asked myself what I was doing. Were these scenes of suffering made to comfort us? I'd cozied up so close to a nice bottle of poison and ebbed away in a glowing eternity of actors and cameras.

Crawling into a bottle looking for a light that isn't there is a spectacular way to put off finding it. I killed the rest of the barrel juice and ended up hanging on a shower rack bawling and begging for mercy from the angels for my prodigality and everything. The rack snapped, of course, and I damn near caved my head in on the rim of the bathtub. I was spared. I put on a foreign film that reminded me of my ex and cried some more. Finally, my phone vibrated. I threw the empty bottle of wine onto the floor where it shattered in a fleeting moment of capricious disgust.

"Who'd want anything to do with a disgusting sack of shit like me? Better they let me rot here alone until I sprout golden teachers out my back," I thought as I answered the phone.

"Yo, I'm outside. You still coming?" It was Jeremy, oh shit. I'd forgotten all about his plans. Thank the heavens I didn't get a robocall.

"Yeah, yeah I'm just getting my pants. I forgot my pants." My voice was trembling.

"Oh, okay," he said. I stepped outside into the evening air. I was soaked from head to toe, which hid the tears streaming down my face. Nobody would believe I was sober so I didn't pretend very hard.

"So where are we going?" I asked, buckling myself in.

"You remember Erik?" asked Jeremy.

"Yeah, of course I do. Big boy."

"Big boy's got a big beach house and big bottles of liquor. He's gone crazy, acting all generous with people he hated a year ago."

"Musta had a breakthrough."

"You betcha. He's gonna be pouring drinks all night till he drops, and he expects us to follow him."

"To oblivion and beyond."

***

Erik's was a beast of a house. Just a few meters from the beach entrance, it had four stories not including the stilted place where his parents' SUVs sat. He got into drugs for the fun of it. When most of his family started soft shunning him, they helped him forget the pain of being a tarnished golden child. His parents were still chill enough to allow him to wreck the place when they were gone, destroying what goodwill they had left for him. The first thing I saw walking in the door was a young man splayed across the marble countertop hugging a bottle of vodka. Someone was trying to pull it out of his hands.

"Ey, ey lay off bro, I'm drinking my beverage here," he yelled.

"You gotta share!"

"Becky wants to drink!"

"Becky, raid the freezer like everyone else!"

"It's EMPTY!" she shouted. With a final tug the young man wrested the bottle from her grip and smacked himself in the face. He tried to sit up and ended up falling off the counter, crushing a chair made of reclaimed driftwood like a house of cards.

I found myself sitting with Erik by a second story window overlooking his pool. I suddenly remembered that we liked each other. I could remember smoking out of aluminum foil pipes behind dumpsters with him. I remembered lying down with complete strangers on his trampoline and hallucinating meteor showers. The nights we smoked were infinitely better than the nights we drank. We always seemed to be out of control in the same way.

"Yeah no... Sherry and I have been at each other's throats ever since she caught me cheating... I guess I can forgive her at some point. It's hard, you know? People keep hitting on me."

"So, you two are like... on a break or something?"

"I don't know what we are. I assume we're on a break. I hope we are anyway." There came the sound of a table collapsing in the other room. "Fuck me..." he muttered under his breath. He took his drink and went to investigate. I got up to puke wherever I could find a bathroom. Erik stopped me on my way down the hall.

"I almost forgot, wanna chug this with me for old times?"

"What's...? Oh, that's nice..." He pressed a glass of PJ into my hands.

"You do half and you do half... I mean, I'll do half and you..."

"...Do half. Cheers."

"You're all right, Jed. You're all right. Have you seen Sherry?" he asked as I downed the entire glass.

"I think she went out to smoke with some people."

"She better not have cut into my stash..." he muttered as he stormed off, not even noticing I'd killed his drink.

***

I woke up on a picnic table by a skating rink. A young gentleman looking no older than nineteen set off down the slopes of a concrete pit and scraped his face on the ground. I pulled myself up and was pleased to see Jeremy and Sherry smiling like grandmothers at me. They were taking turns pulling on a plastic handle of vodka.

"What did I tell you? Nothing like a twenty-minute power nap," he said. I must have passed out and gotten dragged outside for some air. Faint memories of dancing a faux Irish line dance arm in arm with Erik and some guy who made sculptures out of garbage for a living came wafting back as spirits slithered out of my pores. I'd given at least three odes of eternal friendship to people I had never met and would never see again. The taste in my mouth told me that I'd been bumming cigarettes again, tut.

"We decided you needed a little fresh air," said Sherry. I nodded in appreciation and inhaled that good-ass life essence all around. There were at least three visible puke stains in my immediate vicinity. I was beginning to feel the first despairing pangs of a red wine hangover. They offered some of their vodka, which only dressed the aching nausea up in bright tones and dulled its harsher notes. The hangover continued to be a beast despite the potato juice glasses I slipped over the shitshow. At a certain point the buzz began to merge with the roaring hangover, prompting increasingly reckless redosing. I was asleep in the passenger's seat of a taxi on the way home. On arriving Jeremy put on some acid house on full volume. Sherry took the bottle of vodka out of my hands once I'd fished it out of Jeremy's bag and lifted it to her lips. Jeremy stepped out onto the porch before rushing back in, saying:

"I just had the best *fucking* idea y'all, holy shit. Follow, follow." I fell getting off the couch, Jeremy picked me up with one hand and dragged me across the floor with his other wrapped around Sherry, who said, "We should brew some coffee."

***

I woke up on an inflatable raft on the canal.

"You all right there friendo?" he asked. I nodded at Jeremy, smiling. He didn't look nearly as hungover as I must have. "You look like a corpse," he said. "Might wanna cut down."

"I'll die if I ever feel this way again." Despite my honesty, I was still hiding the fact that I felt like a walking corpse already. By the state of my body and my mind, I could tell I was both drunk and hungover.

"How did I get down there?"

"Man, I have to start by saying I did not know you were down there. We were drinking out of coconuts in the kitchen and trying to set up the kief'n'sheesha."

"The what?"

"The kief'n'sheesha. You bought a hookah last night." I slapped my head where my memory of the evening had been deleted. Jeremy showed me indoors. I immediately heard the sound of searing yolk.

"Thank Sherry," said Jeremy, passing me a plate.

"Thanks Sherry. You don't have to, you know."

"I know. I feel bad for using your room while you slept in the canal."

"You slept in my bed?" I asked. Jeremy shrugged, realizing he was involved.

"Sorry, yeah, I hope that's okay," he said. I had a sudden cognition.

"You so you two, like, slept *together*?"

"Kind of, we it was."

"No regrets. Erik's not a part of my life anymore." I swallowed and stabbed another hunk of delicious, buttery joy.

"Did I miss something? I mean y'all do you, I just thought you and Erik were tryna work things out?"

"You *really* need to cut down on your drinking," said Jeremy as he sauntered over to my cabinet to look for the remote. He switched on the flatscreen and sat on the couch. Before the audio kicked in, I saw Erik's face on the local news.

"We're still waiting on word from Sassoon PD about a suspect arrested last night, who is being charged with the negligent discharge of a firearm. We only know that he was heavily intoxicated and 'not thinking clearly' when he pulled the trigger. He is spending his twenty sixth birthday behind bars."

"Oh, sweet Jesus, Erik, what did you do?" I asked.

"You remember when he came up to you?" asked Jeremy.

"No… I really don't." Jeremy sat back on his heels and exhaled deeply.

"Okay, so he wrapped his arm around you and took you to meet his mom and dad in the kitchen. They were on something. I dunno what; they were *geeking* out. They pull you over and pour you some cinnamon whiskey, like half a cup, and you down it in maybe five seconds?"

"I think it was three," said Sherry.

"So, then you say you wanna go chill on the porch with everyone. You barged into this one rotation before you left and started puking halfway to the tree line. Greer was out there shitting himself inside out through his mouth too."

"The other Greer?" I asked. He was the only other kid with my last name at high school. I had always assumed he hated my guts for some reason.

"Yeah you two were getting on like you were, well, family."

"Which…"

"Yeah, so Erik…"

"Oh fuck," I moaned.

"So, building off what the reporter said, he got up on this ping pong table and pulled his little piece out. Then he just started firing randomly into the air. What's so scary is, I was going to tell him that night that I didn't love him anymore. How do you not remember this?" said Sherry.

"Did he hurt anyone?"

"James Fourier lost a little piece of his earlobe."

"Heavenly ol' James? He was there?"

"Yeah. Came out of the woodwork, just wanting to connect with his old classmates. Don't know what made him want to be social with us after what all of us put him through in high school. He was just telling everybody about all the cool shit he's been up to in cyberspace. I'd be surprised if he shows up to the next reunion."

"No kidding. I feel like an asshole."

"We're all assholes. But at least we don't treat guns like toys," said Sherry. We were all motionless for a moment. Jeremy then darted for the eggs still simmering on the stove to save them from burning.

"I'm an asshole though," I said. "I called him an asshole to his face once. I called him a lot of shit. He called me shit too. We fuckin' argued over a damn textbook or some shit…" I felt tears welling up in my face. Jeremy touched my shoulder and gave me an affirming nod as he flipped the pan. "I just want him to know how sorry I am…"

"Put some cheese in there. It really complements the char if you get any," Sherry suggested.

"You got any cheese man?" he asked.

"I have a lot of rum," I replied, wiping water from my eyes. Jeremy looked at me plainly.

"You're not thinking of drinking, today are you? You looked dead out there."

"I wasn't going to. I'm just saying I'm out of cheese."

***

"We got our first performance out of the way, though. We can be happy about that, can't we?" asked Terry from the bathroom. A tacky poster for the Crumpled Bumpkins leaned against their bedroom door. He spat into the sink and replaced his toothbrush. Eve shut her netbook and looked at him.

"*Why* did you quit that job? My dad gave me a call today about it. You know that was embarrassing. Like dude, if you didn't want to work then why the hell did you take the offer?"

"I want to focus on my art. Your Dad had me running all around town all day every day. Whenever I'd get home, I'd be too tired to work on our setlist. Come on, that show we put on was amazing!" Eve shook her head.

"You were high. I got some comments from people saying it sounded like shit."

"That was the best performance I'd given in years! And look, it'd be better if I had the energy to *get* better!" Terry shouted. He sank onto the mattress. "I don't care what people think. My life is my own and I'll spend it how I like." Eve sighed.

"I know you're excited about playing together. I am too. I just need to know that a part of this new start involves you pulling your own weight."

"No problem. I've got plenty of drive. But the art always comes first. That's got to be a part of this too."

5

As soon as Jeremy wasn't there to witness my bullshit, I ditched my mindful morning routine to guzzle down a pint of rum and stare into the dawn until the skyline shook like a leaf in the breeze. My only companions were seagulls, swaying palmettos, and the distant sounds of car trouble. Before long I was wearing the porcelain throne for a dunce cap, howling like Cerberus at the gates of hell. It was a horrendous trade-off for sitting quietly with my own noise and I knew it was before the spirit passed over my lips. There was nobody around, not in the yards across the canal or visible between the stilts of adjacent houses. Some were big enough for three families apiece. I wondered how many of them were rentals.

The sun swelled with color, draped in royal clouds reflecting every one of its ambrosial hues. As some hours passed and my nerves could remember more of themselves and each other, I rose to my feet to stir some bubbling sauce together, a sauce simple in its ingredients and forgiving in its execution, asking only for a firm presence of mind and pardoning the worrisome knife skills of a hungover drunk whose freshman year roommate taught him to cook. I boiled some pasta and let breakfast begin. I had fun despite the crushing sense of despair beneath the buzz I got from cooking. I was almost sad when the time came to sit down and eat. What was there left to do?

I scrolled lazily from news of one dumpster fire to another before turning on the television to watch fictional dumpster fires.

Nothing interested me anymore, but the idea of doing anything seemed aggressive, imperious. My neurotic dithering blended in with the times. Blink, weep, and watch. The only real joy was between me and my breakfast, the screen just made it possible to sit still. When had I last been excited to be graced by its insipid wonders?

As soon as I finished eating, facing a hangover that would last all day, I did what I thought would save my present from its future. I fumbled around the pantry for more canned wine. It tasted like turned apple juice fortified with ever clear wrung out of a bar rag. It was hope, mana of mercy. The invisible hand had escorted the minimum price from eight dollars down to three. The gap in quality was actually beyond words. What was that about expedited means to deteriorated ends?

Booze lobbied for the space I would normally need to fit dinner into my gut. I was ready to pop. A rogue spur could soak the sand under my house with a deep burgundy tint. I felt myself dissolve into a slop of jittering lobes lost in a carnival of cultural delusions, hierarchical daymares, paranoid projections, chemical cravings, obsessive ravings, and silent self-remonstrations. The worm dieth not. Eventually I was plodding, limping really, down the sandy road to the bar to supplement my tailspin with more liquor. I had emptied my den of hope.

There was a flatscreen for every face at Vinny's. A sweet, sweaty dude with dipshit fuckboy energy asked a stranger her name. She gave it. He gave her his, and reached for her hand. She shook it. He turned to look at me and then around. Where did she go? He turned back to me. I waved and smiled. He strode off to a bathroom with the thinnest TP known to human hands. I saw the latent horror in his eyes upon leaving, staring at his fingers, rubbing at spots only he could see.

I began my slide into a Tartarus of ethanol with a few shots of rum, one after the other as per local law. As I became blunted, I couldn't internalize any of the enthusiasm around me at all. I thought of trying tequila. It might prove to be a change of pace, if nothing else. I had come to believe long ago that the hype about its special potency was bullshit; I'd had plenty of regrettable evenings without the stuff. My subsequent memories were connected by a montage of brownout flash cognitions that rang feebly in my head from time to time reminding me that I was alive. If my weakest and most tentative fragments of memory from that time are to be believed, I almost stumbled into a speeding cube car a block away from my house. A cube car.

The next vignette is of lying down next to a bunch of total strangers by a pool. I started passing around cigarettes I found in my pockets and lighting them. I can't recall buying them or picking them up off the dirt. It's entirely possible that I was home, asleep, safe, and sound. There are some dreams we only remember in flashes, glimpses of feeling, a picture where none of the objects can be distinguished from the time and space they occupy, and yet in those instants of recognition we feel we have discovered a life realer and more ours than our own. The next day I was dripping with glimpses like these. These strangers were absolutely wonderful. Their faces bore the marks of patient suffering and final deliverance. They were celebrating something permanent and without intending to, I somehow fell into the center of their collective embrace. I fielded playful questions which I failed to comprehend. My hosts didn't seem to care that my answers made no sense. Bewildered by their kindness, I tried to communicate some gratitude before leaving.

"Paragons of perfect generosity," I blurted out to no response, probably because what I actually said sounded more like: "prgnsprcksmpnity, *hic*." I have a vague memory of my gaze drifting along wooden rafters from a hammock in a big pile with three other people. There was a terrific snap and my back hit concrete. My air got knocked out. Someone struggled to their feet and said we should go. I opened my mouth to respond but nothing came. Nobody knew whose hammock this was. We all sauntered sheepishly home.

"Whatever truth I've found in this life, I sure don't act like I've ever seen it," I said to them as we parted. I never saw any of them again.

***

I woke up in my bed late that afternoon. I stayed there for a few hours as the sun rose. Eventually I stumbled to the sink and drank from the tap. I tried to sleep again but couldn't get past how fucked I felt. I went out and breathed in the drizzling cold on my porch. I still felt too good to be sober. The real hangover was coming but I had time to prepare. I skittered around the kitchen brewing coffee and blue lotus and emptying glass after glass of tap water into my gullet. The deep rot and soreness settled in slowly and without much conviction, but the astonishing cocktail of crippling boredom and anxiety was too much. I couldn't even begin to describe my train of thought; it was everywhere and nowhere. I wandered onto the beach with a copy of The Bell Jar and cried and begged Jesus or Someone to rescue me. The ocean looked dead. In wandering up and down the end's beginning I wondered at the alien I had made of myself.

I then pranced back into Vinny's, which was in the weeds. I dripped all over the bar stool as I repeated my order from yesterday. I allowed the glowing rectangle to steamroll my eyes as I eavesdropped on everyone around me. A monstrous abuse of the senses scaled the heights of my stupor. The tide of inanities flowing from all those screens seemed to menace everyone in the room personally. I envisioned over and over again water laden with jellies and crabs and dogfish spludging into the establishment and soaking my weathered shoes with the greenery of the sea. Only then could I drink as recklessly as I desired.

"You want another one?"

"Yes, thank," I threw back. I was ordering the cheap bourbon. The taste made me want to get sober for good. Unnecessary while the spirit could still force the solution on weak, unwilling flesh. I slammed into someone on my way out the door. He pulled me to the side by the scruff of my neck. He was old, huge.

"Look at me, look at me," he said. I didn't respond. I was too piss drunk at first to recognize he was talking to me. "Is this how you wanna go through life? Is this how you serve your fellow man, how you honor your father, your mother, your own flesh?" I recognized his voice. I looked up into his icon's eyes. His once bright red hair had faded to a wispy gray. His grip, I remember, had lost none of the vigor of his youth. He was wearing a collared shirt with a logo that said 'the Millennial Congregation.' "Do you know who I am?"

"Emmanuel M. Hutch."

"How do you know that?" He dropped me. I backed away a step to grab what was left of my drink.

"You're Terry's uncle." A spiritual entrepreneur if there ever was one, Hutch had founded more religions than most people join in a lifetime.

"Oh. I was hoping you were a student of my work."

"I've seen your work." He paused for a moment, guessing at my meaning.

"Buy you a coffee?" he asked. So, I sat out with him in the drizzle and he asked me about Terry.

"Yeah, he's back in town."

"Did he ask you for money?" Hutch asked, his upper lip steeped in brew.

"He just wanted a place to stay for a while."

"I don't know why he didn't just come home." I winced. Hutch was Terry's only remaining family. He was afraid to go home to him after school since the 3rd grade. For a moment, all the anger in my heart died. "What's he doing now?" he asked.

"He's got a band."

"Another one? What's it called?"

"…Actually, I dunno."

"I thought he would consider a new career. It doesn't look like California was very kind to him."

"It's what he's good at. It beats selling pills for a charlatan," I said. Hutch looked me blank in the face before swiping my mug off the table. Shards slid across the outdoor dining area. Once again, I was craning my neck up at him. He adjusted his collar and called me a fuckup. As he strutted off, I went for more shots. I felt good. I felt really good. There was no depth to fathom, no realization, no attainment. There was only the disturbing sensation that everything was okay, even when it wasn't.

***

Jeremy picked me up for breakfast.

"Meaningless ol' Hutch boozin' at Vinny's, whodathunkit," he said, munching away at an omelet. I stabbed a pickle.

"It's fucked, man. I throw away so much money at that bar and most of the time I come away feeling like shit," Jeremy nodded patiently and looked me in the eye while he drained his plastic glass of sweet tea.

"That's life. Sometimes you go out and someone slaps you on the back and covers your tab and sometimes you just get your head bitten off."

"Nobody has ever covered my tab. Never."

"Really?" He pushed a little pile of salt around with his insulting finger. It could have been because of the acute impact of an early morning hangover, but for whatever reason I wondered what his fingers would feel like in my mouth. He called over the waitress and paid for my food.

"Let's go see Gabriela!"

***

I'd known Gabriela since my sophomore year of high school, when one afternoon she convinced the principal to vote for her favorite candidate when he playfully decided to debate her, explaining the connection between racist state violence and capitalism. She came to prefer sculpture over other arts to shape the world around her.

We pulled up to her house on the mainland. It rose three stories, a marble crown by a pond of swans. We found her father in the kitchen slicing what looked like an entire garden. He rounded the kitchen isle and put his shoulder around Jeremy.

"Where have you been?" he asked, cracking a smile I remembered from Gabriela's valedictorian speech.

"Work, mostly."

"Gabriela told me you were applying for postgraduate education." Jeremy laughed at that.

"That all sorta fell through," he said.

"She's downstairs, make yourselves at home," Gabriela's mother called from the living room as we took our shoes off. She was reading a commentary on the I Ching.

"I didn't know you'd be back so early! How was your trip?" asked Jeremy. Her mother sighed.

"A speaker at the convention died very suddenly. He was the only one at the table who was adequately prepared to speak on such a narrow topic…"

"What was that?"

"A proposed grammar of a language isolate spoken near his university. Even the understudy he brought with him struggled to read his mentor's handwriting. That poor young man had to wing the entire talk. After that long layover in Monrovia and the flight over, I'm surprised I'm not asleep right now."

"She's been awake thirty-six hours now. It's that book she's writing keeping her up," said Mr. Nwaigbo.

***

Gabriela finished off the roach, leaned her head back, and let forth a column of white smoke.

"Are you alive?" asked Jeremy. She returned to us.

"Domain, kingdom, phylum, class, order, family, genus, species, subspecies. Age, epoch, period, era, eon."

"You smoke a lot," I said.

"Not as much as you. No offense but your lungs are not ashtrays," she replied.

"That's true." I leaned back on her couch and took in her music. "This sounds a bit like the Crumpled Bumpkins," I said.

"I could offer you some recipes, Jed. Maybe so you breathe a little easier?" offered Jeremy. I took this in. I never intended to become a regular smoker and since I became one, I never really sat back to think just how long I'd been overdoing it. It hurt to breathe.

"Okay, yeah."

"Speaking of the Bumpkins, how are they? I heard they had a little trouble moving in," asked Gabriela.

"The Crumpled Bumpkins? How the fuck should I know?" asked Jeremy.

"Dude, they literally live right next to you." There was a pause.

"Eve and Terry are the Crumpled Bumpkins?" I asked. Gabriela doubled over laughing.

"Are you that dense? I'm sorry, I love you, I don't mean to offend, but holy *shit*. How did you not know that? Jeremy, Eve gave me those tickets specifically so you would go and recognize them. Do you think I'm just out here buying tickets and giving them away?"

"I mean, they were wearing masks. Are we supposed to recognize mascots under their masks?"

"You didn't recognize anything about their sound, their setup, anything?" We all sat with that.

"Jeremy told me you gave him some DMT," I said.

"I got *lucky* with that connection. It's kept the last few months interesting, like *really* interesting. I'm making stuff now I couldn't have dreamt of before. My parents even know I smoke it now and then and they're totally chill. Did you want some by the way?" she asked, drifting over to the drawer where she kept it.

"You know, I..."

"He's still pretty skittish around psychedelics."

"Still? Really?"

"My set's not right. I'm hung up on failure. I'm pretty sure all I'd find is a nightmare."

"Hey, that's fair. No pressure. I will say though, if you can put away your fear of death and failure for just... fifteen minutes, you might discover a whole new way to look at your situation. Sometimes the only way to raise your spirits is to give up the ghost."

6

Jeremy and I drifted in and out with the waves, pushing and pulling with the sea. My eyes were bolted to the clouds. I didn't hear Gabriela weaving among the dunes to join us.

"Drinks?" asked Jeremy, asking her and I in turn.

"As agreed," affirmed Gabriela. We wore sunlight on our shoulders before sloughing it off in exchange for the fluorescent illumination of the gas station. "Oh shit... He's back!" she pointed. I looked to my left and saw a familiar shuffling of feet. It was Sir John alone transcribing something onto a damp notepad, probably direct from source. The sea inspired him as it lashed at what remained of his evening wear. I excused myself and went down to him, "Do you wanna welcome him back for us? I'm parched," asked Jeremy.

"We'll wait for you by the air pump," said Gabriela. I bowed and went over to the haggard young gentleman. I hopped over a berm and got my feet wet next to his.

"Where'd you go?" I asked.

"Tried to escape," he muttered.

"Where to? Why?"

"Bullshit places and bullshit reasons everywhere. I should do as Lao Tzu instructs: prefer what is within to what is without."

"...Were you visiting an ex?"

"I canceled plans to meet with old friends too. Naturally she was even more disgusted by what I'd become than I ever was of her and changed her mind after polishing off my wine." He turned to face me for the first time in two years. "How are you?"

"I don't feel right," I replied.

"Why's that?" he asked.

"Only time I feel normal is when I drink."

"So, you're chemically dependent or there's something in your life you can't stand. Maybe it's both. Maybe something you think you can't change has you self-medicating to function. I've been there: coke, heroin, fentanyl, meth, the occasional dab binge. You're a little tit on a big bleeding sow. The sober are outnumbered in dying dreams and the calm are even fewer."

"I'm starting to realize my life is slipping by and it's not how I want it to be. The days slip by, one and the same haze. I've accepted the haze concealing a place I never intended to create. It's my fault, but the weight of it doesn't lighten with my admission. I'm twenty-three and I've done nothing, that or something worse. At this point I'm terrified I'll reveal a mind irrevocably damaged by a lifetime of escapism in a job interview and cease to fucking exist right there. I'm worried there is nothing left of me for me or anyone else to fix." I said. His big bleary eyes blinked.

"No choice. I followed the straight path as I knew it. I made concessions that made me a monster. I lost everything I nurtured into life. I got to my feet here, broke and stranded in paradise, taking everything that came my way on the road. America's frying, my friend. The island of lotus-eaters chewed me up and spat me out because I couldn't stomach the fruit."

"You mean like from The Odyssey?"

"I'm talking about the modern lotus island of stucco, stone, concrete, timber, and glass. We have brutalized nature and have become frightened of it and ourselves. We retreat to a new nature of our own making to shape us in ways we cannot see, lovingly tending to the machines that tend to us as mother perishes. What have we traded for our Gaia? Most of what we make is owned by someone else before we make it. Our eyes stray not outside the screen. Our feet stray not outside our walls. Our hands stray not outside the lines. If we can choose what we have on our screen, we call that freedom. We don't miss the wide world, its food, its faces, its people and tongues. We aspire for bigger boxes and better screens to bury the sentimental world of wandering attention beneath once and for all. Peering through fake windows at a fake cosmos blacked out and weary, we accept death without guessing that life might have asked something of us had we the courage to meet it for once. The machines have freed us that we may adore them forever and that is all they saved us for."

"I hear what you're saying," I said.

"There's no 'Sir John' to possess oblivion. Behold! Be! Even drifting I'm still not free of mother plastic, of sweet electricity ambrosia, of the embrace of ephemeral deliriums in order to accept that life is one of many. This does not perfect you over others trapped in the web. You can be freed of anything in particular, but never from the need to be free. I don't want to discourage you. The bright side is the unspoken part."

"It's been two years since the breakup. Every day since has circled the same drain. Every day I'm trying to feel something new, only in the same exact way."

"Because you're embalmed, right?"

"Right."

"You see, it's pulling you along just to kick you in the ass. 'Drink and you'll forget how bad the last binge stung.' Do you see how an attachment like that regiments the hell out of life? Even if you're attached to letting go, that will *still* leave you bound up and scrambling for leverage. I can't help but think that drink, instead of handing you the keys to your freedom, just replaces your old dilemmas with new ones. You may prefer those problems over the ones you have when you're sober, even if you're spitting up blood. That is a terrifying reality to face, but remember: just as attachment is inevitable, so is change."

"I have to pull myself out of this well. I'm worried I don't have what it takes to get out. I'll just fall, crack my head and drown. If I stay at the rock bottom, sure there's no reward but there's no risk either." A clot of reeds washed up on the shore. A fiddler crab scuttled by.

"Of course, then you're just sticking your head under the mud. What's worse than that?" Sir John asked.

"Just being at the helm, having to choose to make your life worth something is like pulling teeth."

"I could call you childish for that attitude, but I know that's not fair. I think you know you're at the helm whether you acknowledge it or not. A non-decision is still a decision. To turn away from what's hurting you, you must believe that you are already worth salvaging."

"What keeps you from going back to the things that hurt you? Is it your lodge? Are they super encouraging?" I changed the subject.

"No, things at the lodge are pretty… acrimonious right now. The rumor mill's been spinning off its hub. The cliques and recriminations are a headache. We'll sort it out, but I'm not necessary so I stay out here," he sighed. He threw his arms up in frustration. "The truth is, by now there's nothing left to go back to. Nothing can imprison you forever, not even your own body or your own mind. It all rots, like that dead shark over there. It all feeds source and soil. We're bound to the snares of life just as we're bound to *escape them,* Jedediah. Your old problems might well vanish before you ever get the nerve to solve them. Whether we solve our problems or face them, we can never know who we will become, what in the end was worth solving. We are free to choose. We think of transcendence as the ivory tower, when all feats are accomplished and all conundrums are resolved. But real freedom comes when the iron tower collapses into the detritus of the banks of this ocean with our name. Only then are we unbound. Only then are we free to begin again. Imagine the eons that have passed into that muck! And here we are, grateful to the furnace of the ages for bringing us and all we love around! *That, the acceptance of that, is the medicine you need,*" he said as he sat down on the sand, digging his fingers in and churning up an enormous glop of Earth.

"I'll think about that. Thanks, Sir John."

"Peace be upon you," he said. I walked to the pier and found my two companions leaning on a pillar by the tide.

"Jesus, Jed, did he give you the sermon on the mount?"

"Not this week," I smiled.

"What now?" asked Jeremy.

"I've got an idea," said Gabriela.

***

The three of us thanked the bearded gentleman holding Kasino's door open for us. Once again into that maze of couches we crept, dark except for the blacklight making the place look like a jellyfish enclosure. I looked around and found almost everyone there in one of a million states of dissolution. The indiscriminate mixture of coffee, nicotine, and cheap vodka provided at the bar couldn't explain what we saw. There were a number of other chemical culprits involved in the freakouts, fights, and fugues all around us. Peering past clouds transforming like squid ink in the neon murk, I could see a forbidden pharmacy being insufflated, popped, vaporized, and injected. That's not to mention all the spiked pastries and stinging gummies people were shoving into their faces just a little too discreetly. The staff was indifferent to everything short of a major ass-beating so long as the ATF industry operations investigator wasn't considering one of his rare visits.

There were legal highs to supplement whatever got smuggled in. There were people going up to the counter time and again for their diminishing returns. The hookah smokers chugged along without an approved ventilation system overhead. A duo of obsessive drinkers offered authentic absinthe to the bartender. The dancing throng spilled over their tiny floor and frequently knocked shit over. A circle of hobbyists held hands as one of their number smoked salvia extract from a wooden pipe. It's only in the places where anything goes that anything can happen. Breathing in the smog of chemicals alone disarmed our senses before we could even order anything. Incredible, the air alone had a corrosive effect on the barrier between events and the people experiencing them. What was in that haze? Nothing I'd ever heard of.

***

When we all started getting nauseous, we went outside to sway in the breeze. The streetlight's glare featured colors it wasn't supposed to. I took two steps to the car to see if I could throw up somewhere private. Jeremy stopped me, "Whoa there, you almost fell." I nodded at him and stepped back a scoche. Then I heard a thwack from behind. Gabriela had tripped on the curb. Jeremy stooped to help her up.

"You okay there?" I mumbled as I took two steps forward again and tripped over a parking bar. My chin hit the asphalt. It took me a moment to register that my teeth should have shattered, but I was a little more relaxed about the whole thing than I should have been.

"Fuck, we're dropping like flies out here…" Jeremy cussed and grabbed my elbow and helped to stuff my body in the car. Gabriela slumped onto the passenger's seat and we bolted, feeling that we had somehow dishonored ourselves. I dry heaved a few times but somehow convinced my stomach not to ruin Jeremy's leather seats.

* * *

I came across Sir John again an hour past sunrise. He was up to his calves in water. I waded up to him.

"What're you doing?" I asked.

"Looking for horseshoe crabs. I know they're out here, the little angels."

"What'cha want with 'em?"

"Just to look. I think there is hardly a more beautiful thing on this Earth than a horseshoe crab."

"You think so?"

"The universe unfolds by the grace of a tactful asymmetry. By our being inflected with the unexpected we come to our many ends, among them is the honor of stillness within motion. To be at utter repose with oneself and one's world through ages upon ages of anger and tribulations while in unceasing motion, unceasing celebration, is the reward the horseshoe crab experiences simply for going about its way. Its mannerisms are not simply appropriate or polite, far exalted above such words are such humble and beautiful ways as this blessed being! Imagine, Jedediah, look and *see* the regal qualities of a form that persists for *420 million years!*"

"Hm."

"I'm serious, consider them! Why, if I could do anything this side of the grave, it'd be to show people the beauty that's hidden in plain sight." With a graceful motion he plucked the husk of a horseshoe crab out of the sand and handed it to me underside up. I held it for a moment and noticed how the delicate curvature of its carapace razored out into serrated ends. "By the way, I had a volume of my aphorisms printed off just recently. I was going to give you a copy, but I understand if your reading list is full at the moment," he said. I shook my head as if to say I had nothing going on. He pulled a thin paperback volume out of his tote bag. I accepted it from him with a nod. I turned to the first page and squinted for a moment. This is what I saw:

Sevlesruo rof ti peek ton yam ew tub, sevlesruo ti evig yam dna, efil nevig era ew. Erofeb neeb reven evah yeht sa erom ecno gnirps evol yrev taht dna egdelwonk yrev taht dna, wena sgnirps efil sa dehsinotsa era ew neht dna, su morf nrot si evol dna wonk ew gnihtyreve sa hctaw ew. Gniyfirret woh dna lufrednow woh, egnahc, lufrednow woh.

I looked up at him.

"Are they all like that?"

"Oh no, I thought that one would just be a fun little gimmick."

"Mhm."

***

At that time, I felt I constituted a sad low for the human artifact. At the ass end of millions of years of desiccating air, cooling winters, and dwindling herds was the great and plentiful slump of the Anthropocene. All that time, energy and wits were the price of food. Industry changed the price, and the cost came to energy and wits. Comfort had undone what the rigors of nature could not. I'd never been so weak, unsure, or distracted. Sure, I'd slept under a tarp and the ocean of stars before. That didn't change the fact that I was an outgrowth of the shrink-wrap kingdom. As months and years dragged on my skin and guts would slide off the brittle wireframe that held them close. I would ultimately be confirmed in my course, lost to a featureless blue, alien to the sky and the sea, living my life in fear of a world I no longer know.

A seagull stole a joint from me once. The next morning, I caught it staring at me through the window when I was just brewing my business and minding my coffee. It could have been another scoundrel, but at that moment I was sure it was him. In his eyes I saw bottomless hunger from a time without ice caps, without winters, when forests were ever green and prey were plentiful as the grass that had yet to evolve. In that frayed morning hour that gaze from that dumpy little dinosaur reminded me that the Anthropocene was an epoch of tragic decline. I saw something deeper in the eyes of a dead fish on the dock, the memory of a time still more chaotic and incomprehensible. I lived near the abyss of the sea anticipating the abyss of death. The empty eyes of the bleeding wahoo knew both.

A glut of trash turgidly flowed down the canal that week. There was the usual fare of beer bottles, fruit skins, various lengths of spine, and other weird shit. I'd never seen a kid passed out on a float in the canal before. There he was slung, dead to the world, along the back of an inflatable goose sliding across the water. He looked like Marat in his bathtub, only red as a lobster. He couldn't have been more than nineteen. I tossed a beer onto the float and went indoors and didn't come out for the rest of the day. My phone had been dead for two days. Not even that frenzied little brick could violate the sanctity of the nest.

***

The next evening Jeremy and I were back at the pizza shack to discuss this or that. Apparently, Jeremy saw Eve and Terry the minute we walked in. He stiffened up a little, then pretended to relax. I, having imbibed irresponsibly before hitting the bar, didn't notice either of them until Eve approached me as I stumbled to the bathroom to puke.

"I'm sorry about showing up at your place. I should've just asked or something. It's just — *you* blocked me on *everything*. For *what?* Am I that–Anyway, I would have–I *would* have had Terry tell you we were coming but *he* said —"

"Look, it really doesn't matter. I'm honestly happy for you two. We're square; I don't care," I said. She winced at that.

"You know, I was scared to move back here. You're some of the only people I know here and it hurts that I'm supposed to pretend to be happy while you shun me."

"What should I do, unfuck our relationship?"

"We shouldn't be strangers," she said. Terry waved awkwardly from behind her.

"Neither of you are strangers, but right now I'd just like to be alone," I said, moving along slowly.

"Do you want to live the rest of your life like this? Avoiding everything and everyone? Life goes by like that, Jed. What if you regret being alone?"

"I already regret this conversation." I walked past her and threw up into the toilet. On flushing and walking out I said, "I care about you both. I don't like how I'm taking anything right now. Can I say though, that the least of what I need is a little more condemnation from you? I want to be far away from you. That's all."

"Do you think I came here to hurt you? I'm here to be *happy*. That's all. If you're still hung up on shit I did years ago then that's… that I guess. You should know I'm way past forgiving *your* mistakes. Maybe it's time you did the same, Jed." Jeremy nodded in the corner as he ordered a beer. I looked at him. Eve winced and said, "I just thought you'd appreciate someone looking past the fact that you're a burnout, since nobody else does. But you're not gonna do that, are you? You're just going to shun me like when you two were sleeping around behind my back?" she said, pointing at Jeremy grimacing at the taste of an IPA.

"For the record, I thought you two were already splitsies," he muttered from across the room.

"You walked in on us!" she protested.

"I wasn't aware you had to have a *thing* to hatefuck," he said. I tried not to laugh. After draining his drink to the last drop, he slammed his glass down and switched to liquor. Eve looked more sad than angry.

"Maybe he knows you better than I ever did. I'm just saying I give a shit about you too. I hate this… *wall* of silence everyone puts up around here so they don't have to deal with the mistakes they made when… when we knew we'd never see each other again. I've never written anyone off in my *life*. I'm done pretending like *this* part of my life doesn't matter to me," she paused, calculating. "You can hate me all you want but I'm done letting you —" she stopped herself, "I'm done letting that dictate how I live. This is my hometown too." I'm not sure if either she or I knew what she wanted to convey. I looked down at my knees and said,

"I don't hate you," and shuffled over to join my friend. Eve sat down at Terry's booth with a sigh I was meant to hear, more disappointed than angry.

"Fuck your gambaw," someone called loudly across the room. All three of us turned to look. It was some disheveled mess of a man drooling on himself in a corner, decked out in an amazing suit with matted bronze hair draped all over his slender face. He seemed no older than twenty-five. He was face down on the table, looking like shit. I'd never seen someone deeper in the drink. Eve turned to me with a cautious smile and said:

"I have to hand it to you though, at least you're not *that* guy." The man belched and leaned back into perfect slumber. A massive pan at his table suggested he'd eaten an extra-large pizza in a single sitting. "Looks like he's had enough whiskey to kill a hog."

"To be real though, I think I *have* been that guy." That made Jeremy chuckle. Terry and Eve chuckled after him, trying to strike up some synergy. The world had not been kind to them. Numb though I was, their isolation and estrangement were as clear to me as my own.

"Holy shit… I know this guy," Jeremy said. He got out of his seat, broadening his normally slender shoulders, approaching the disheveled one. "Shaw? Is that you?" he whispered. Shaw, or whoever he was, had no response. An exhausted employee came by to grab his empty pan and kicked him gently in the shin.

"Ey, ey, you can't sleep in here bro. I told you last time." Shaw glared through the man.

"Hey, are you Shaw Schleisinger?" asked Jeremy. Shaw looked at him. There was no recognition in his eyes. His head sank onto the table.

"Let's leave him be, man," said Terry. Eve placed a water bottle gentle by the drunkard's side.

Eventually I shook my head and invited everyone to the same table. Before I even knew what was happening, we were talking like we'd never been apart. The conversation flowed on fine, mostly because I had nothing to say. Terry bought us drinks and I thanked him. We downed them together. I didn't realize this at the time, but one day I would miss every single one of those faces exactly as they were then. I would miss the shabby clothes I wore and the feeling that except for those three people I was completely and utterly alone.

We all walked out onto the beach and looked at the stars wink at us. The relentless wind and the moonless dark kept most off the beach. We remembered to each other ill adventured beach restoration projects of the murky past and being beaten down by Septober waves. Jeremy just stared out into the water. We saw someone march past us into the waves. He was wearing pastel blue shorts that hiked up far over his knees. His polo shirt was streaked with vomit. He tried to look up at the moon and stumbled backwards onto his ass. I went up to him and tried to help him up.

"Where are your friends?" I asked. He swayed on his feet, foundations giving way. A limp arm rose to indicate the beach exit. Then he collapsed onto the sand. Jeremy huffed angrily and walked home while we looked around for help.

"Let his friend take care of him!" he shouted.

"They all left him out here like this," Eve protested.

"Well he's got shitty taste." As Jeremy said this, the young beachgoer's friends actually showed up.

"I found him!" called the vanguard to the others. A whole crowd came to escort their drunken man-child away.

***

Eve ride-shared us back to the apartment building where the majority of us were staying. The trip was mostly silent. Despite some tension, there was an inescapable impression that the night had gone well.

"Are we friends again?" Eve asked. She was smiling.

"We were always friends," I lied.

"Me too?" asked Terry. I looked at him and nodded.

"What the fuck were you two thinking?" I asked.

"When?"

"When you… showed up at my house without telling me you were together first. What were you thinking?"

"I guess… I mean it's like… A part of me was afraid of telling you, another part assumed you didn't care, another part was… sort of mad that you probably *wouldn't* care… so I was able to just kinda put any second thoughts away," said Eve.

"You didn't think I'd care?"

"There were so many variables, how was I really supposed to know? I focus and I focus and… Jesus, Jed, I'm fucking sorry. I'd been *moving* and *depressed* and… is it okay that for once I fucked up?"

"For once?"

"Fuck you, you know what I mean," Eve said, laughing.

***

Four years before that conversation, I was visiting Eve at her university across the border. Someone was screaming outside. All yesterday's parties were finally over. We could stop pretending to be fancy. She was trying to sleep off the champagne on my chest. Her fingers found marks on my shoulder.

"You never told me about these."

"I said they were burn marks."

"But you never told me how you got them."

"After that fight we had two weeks ago…"

"The one where you told me you didn't love me or the one where I told you I was leaving you for Ralph?"

"The other one. I drove to some supermarket parking lot and put matches out on myself."

"...What?"

"Yeah... I was upset. I don't know why I did it exactly, only that I couldn't stand what was going through my head."

"Why didn't you tell me about this?"

"I was afraid you'd react badly." She sat still for a moment. Then she sat up and started getting dressed.

"Did I say something wrong?"

"How do you think I'm supposed to react to that information?"

"Safe...ly?" I suggested. She rubbed the line in her forehead.

"It's like I can't trust you anymore."

"What?" I asked, making a move to console her.

"Stop. I can't. I just need to process — Oh my fucking god why did you do that?"

"Hey, it's not like I'm not ashamed of myself! That's why I didn't fucking tell you!"

"This *concerns* me, Jed. My Dad always told me if some guy was emotionally blackmailing me..."

"Blackmailing? What? I felt bad. It's a coping mechanism. Yeah, maladaptive but... I never meant for you to find out."

"I can't believe you just go around acting like everything's okay with you when you have all... *This* in you! I can't trust you!"

"I really don't like how this conversation is going. Let's start over and —"

"If I make you so miserable then why did you drive down here? Why are you wasting my time? Your time? Instead you make the drive anyway, calling me halfway to bitch at me about traffic and taking hours longer than you should! What do you even get out of being here?"

"I love you," I said. We argued for a few more hours. Then we drank to forget that we fought and pretended to lay down our arms. I knew that exchange was toxic as hell. It's just that, at the time, I needed to feel wanted. I would have put up with anything, no matter how damaging in the long run, just to have been wanted.

I dreamt I was sticking my own fingers with a fork that night. They bobbed in a little brain-case'o'broth. I could hardly wait to chew every bite, breaking my own bones in convulsions of pleasure. I woke up screaming as the last tendon gave way. She asked what's wrong. I lied. She and I argue about the meaning of the dream I lied about having, something about a goat. We yawned and held each other until dawn. The argument resumed when her roommate came home and found our bedroom door ajar. We sat up, covering our shame, getting chewed out for the shitshow in plain sight. We had forgotten our bottle of pinot noir, balancing it perfectly at the edge of the stove. We were set to work clawing its rosy bits into a bag, the broth now blooming over the varnish-scuffed wooden floors as a portent of our souring minds.

7

We are delivered to this earth not all at once but in layer after quaking layer all mythologizing themselves out of confusion. Like the innocent impaled on a pipe sticking out of the swelling tide, we find that the new era is suddenly upon us. We are torn from our communities and our flesh is torn from us, born again from the ruptures of history. The body and mind molds to the new reality, snaps in place or snaps itself. We are delivered in bloody stages, patties on patties, human flesh, and served for those who would sample the mess.

 Terry was seventeen when he found three or four tabs of lab grade LSD exposed under his brother's bed in a lockbox wrapped up in a garbage bag full of rotting fruit for just anyone to claim. Nursing a precocious interest in the pharmacology of psychedelics, he researched the drug thoroughly beforehand. He then proceeded to ignore the advice he collected from old heads all over the web, credulous as a Victorian naturalist tottering into a UFO. Dearly Benighted Uncle Hutch's Millennial Congregation, a heresiarchy spawned from the Apophatic Academy cast in the image of an open pharmatopia of the sage junky's sweetest nods, would witness his unmaking and his rebirth.

 He remembered his brother and his Uncle's bringing him onboard their obscenely profitable psychoactive crusade some months before. Terry understood at that point that what he was dropping was a safer alternative to the backlog of legal highs languishing in boxes all around him. A thick silence coated everything, distorting the world within and without the compound. The deep and dismal depths of the sand-soiled forest frightened him at night. He always expected the explosive hiss of something too big to be a dog. The lake promised eternity in death.

He sat meditating in the middle of his room for half an hour and lapped the entire steal into his gullet. He thought he could taste something at first something oddly metallic but figured it was just the paper. He remembered pathologically persistent psychonautic bulletins that LSD shouldn't taste like shit. He felt the little pieces warp soundlessly between his teeth and granted access to the glow. He put some music on, laid back, and waited. Within twenty minutes he sat up and looked around his living little room, as if for the first time. His personal effects stood so stark by the bare wall. They didn't seem different, but they were new. He rose up and drifted buoyantly out the door.

He stepped out into the undulating hallway and passed his brother's Spartan accommodations into the auditorium. Its great walls heaved heavenward. It frowned with a regal curve too perfect to glare with such malice. At one end was a view of the intracoastal waterway in all its unspeakable beauty. At the other was the blank stage before rows of empty couches. He could picture Hutch strutting up and down before a crowd of twenty or thirty people, sweating, gesticulating, heaving his arms into the air in great leaps of logic, beating his own face bloody for effect, and cursing the audience for not having thought to come to him sooner. That was before the bite. The police would come around to check in, but they could never find a law discussing any of the powders and potions confiscated from the Congregation hall.

Familiar faces squeezed their taxidermy zoetrope shows from suppurating wounds of holy light, drawing tears with desolate appeals for pity that only inspired confusion and terror in the boy. He thought about the accident. He thought of the faces of his parents consumed by fire. The gaping jawbones framed the lips that kissed him to sleep just the other night were erupting with tongues of flame. He and his brother went from a life of love and comfort to Hutch's dead hive. Terry felt the man's pride and miserable isolation melded in a loveless marriage. Who the hell took anything seriously? Terry met horror when he met his Uncle and realized that a man so powerful and so careless walked free. Though coherent as radio static, his essential feel for the Molochian control that surrounded him was absolute. There was no reason for any of it. Hutch had never healed or helped anyone, not even himself, so far as Terry could remember. Yet, even when the pews were empty Hutch mounted the stage and gave them a sermon for the ages. He was playing the same sick game just as hard if not harder than everyone else, the game of replacing fallible flesh with a shell of gold and stone and status. Did he know that he was playing the game? Is that what separated him from the other sick fucks not in on the open secret? But when he interrogated himself on the matter, he found nobody to consult. He cried in the way. Everyone knew what no-one could say.

Why didn't the ascended master descend among his parishioners and allow another ward of God to speak? What special sense entitled him to others' unswerving faith? Terry laughed in amazement. The world was bleeding to death under the purview of a bunch of entitled adult children. The message was clear. Nothing can be lifted any closer to the ground of being. We are all here together. He couldn't believe the audacity of spotless, prideful hierarchs damning themselves with their pretenses of holiness any longer. The haunting attachment of the lifer to the legal treadmill of tweaking legal highs, chasing a nostalgia remixed every three months with a random perk or liver disease to ignore, filled him with contempt for the man giving them a reasonably extortionate price for it. In donning a mantle of spurious wisdom, he got them to disown their authentic experience of reality. What kind of wisdom demands underlings? To the countless few who love others as themselves, who rarely make history but who live in everyone, may they steer clear of Emmanuel.

He had waited his whole life to find out that the light of truth was the apple of all, equally. A joy like the sight of pearly gates killed him time and again. The whole world could know! He extasized over his martyrdom in countless technicolor fantasy plays before kicking open the front door. This was his great commission! He needed to heed the voice of God, to lose himself to the truth in as reckless and *fun*... no, *truthful* way as possible. He needed the anointing light. It was his birthright! He would ensure it was hallowed in all corners of the world before the light of his awareness dimmed, while he could still swim the deep waters. He cautiously fumbled with his phone and a speaker he'd retrieved from the fruit-bag. He held the humming plastic to his chest and became a purr of sound. Within twenty minutes he was totally convinced he was dead. Hopelessly adrift, he dissolved into garbage, into the luminous, marvelous, and endless abyss of ordinary bullshit, the carnivorous plant that loved him and would kill him someday.

Life and death spooled him into their impenetrable weave, until all tales of birth and ashes were a blazing abyss. It was hours before any form, figure or voice was able to untangle itself from searing and unsearchable totality. He wept bitterly to think he'd been hornswoggled by the lie of his own birth. He rubbed his temples, trying to figure out what he was going to do about the great con. Each and every splash of self-interest and self-awareness burned like boiling grease on his back. He marveled with fingers clasped fast to his elbows, kneeling before the coming dawn, flinching at the insinuations of silhouettes and stars no matter how dim or far. Whether his eyes were open or closed, his was a land flowing with mountainous morphogenetic mythopoetic smorgasbords. His heart trembled. It was as though all the delicate pieces of his soul had been smashed out for analysis by the hammer of an unspeakable god to be put back together as something equally unspeakable. He stared up into a glittering hell of lilting quartz gesticulating at him from up above the ceiling fan. He despaired like one drowning in a coffin. It was the beginning.

After hours of patient suffering, he remembered his great commission. The quest to forge a new monad was still at hand. This new purpose cleansed him of despair. The splendid sight of imago dei reflected in the windows all around spurred him on. He donned a bathrobe and set forth on his journey. He went door to door inviting people to accept the truth they already knew. For the most part nobody even came to the door. The few who did either took him to be some kind of occultic salesman or a gurning hiker in need of directions. Though he never got through to anyone, he knew that they knew. Everyone knew, they always had and they always would.

Dehydrated and sober enough to recognize it, Terry decided to find his way home. The pain had gone from a heroic endorphine soaked memento mori to the agony of his young life. He knew he would never be the same. Psychedelics could quicken dormant mental illnesses in those with predispositions. Would his anxieties spiral out of control? Would he retreat into isolation? Would he find it difficult to relate to his peers? His bizarre prophecies began fulfilling themselves.

As the trip waned, he lay flat on his back listening to minutes of zesty, decaying ballroom music in his bedroom in the dead of night. It was so ornate, so original, so hilarious that it kept him completely immersed. He went to turn up the volume. The speaker was dead. He realized that this delightful music was a daydream in his eardrum peeking out the ambience of a settling house, pipes of hot water, and the swamps stewing outside. He had symphonies within him, how would he let them out?

Eve thought he'd jilted her by the time it took him to face smartphones again. Feeling trapped, he avoided attachment in the only town he ever knew. He avoided her and he avoided me. He avoided everything because he was planning to leave. It wasn't just the wasteland under Hutch's thumb he wanted to leave behind. Sassoon itself was a drag. Had this not happened, I doubt Eve would've reached out to me in quite the way she did.

I can't say Terry changed all at once. It's hard to tell you're not you anymore. Self-concept by its nature resists the changes that come naturally to body and mind with the plenitudes and penalties of age. His experience put his little life in sharp relief with the eons. He didn't belong anywhere. He didn't know anything. As overcome or as relieved as he might have been at the impermanence of everything in his life, his most important realization was that his toxic ties to his Uncle were temporary. He drifted a little further off. He prepared to sacrifice everything he'd ever known for a chance to be free. When he sailed into the open road for the first time, screamed and wept for joy. He skipped his senior year entirely.

***

The last real scare of the evening came when Terry's brother returned late at night with Hutch from an unprofitable misadventure that beggared description. Terry thought they would see his dilated pupils and seething, suppurating aura and make assumptions. Just before they reached his hallway he stole into his room and escaped through the window. He skipped over the gravel parking lot to the trees. He wondered what it would be like to go to Church on Sunday, believe every word the pastor said, and ride home with his believing family to digest small town gossip and eat burgers off the grill before football. That had never been his life. Emmanuel was the last of their kin, who adopted them in the year-long interval when he was a Baptist preacher between founding the Apophatic Academy and the Millennial Congregation.

When the Baptist venture failed, he eventually resorted to making up for the lost tithes by selling religious experiences in vials. This was around the time Terry came into the picture. The literature got progressively more unreadable as Hutch snorted increasingly obscure powders, vaporized ever weirder analogues and derivatives, and swallowed a barrel of gelatinous nootropics to think of ways to advertise their effects to people. As Hutch went on autopilot into a wormhole of exploitation and polyaddiction, his nephews maintained an online vendor for gray market pharmaceuticals. Whenever Terry handled a transaction online, he was supposed to tell clients that the truth was in the pills, the books were more for decoration. This was a way to excuse the quality of the books. One sacrifice that Hutch actually made for his charges was being the guinea pig for his own products. Terry was forbidden to sample anything for himself. Terry looked over the place where his life had become affixed and silently wept.

***

Jeremy sat still in a cube of glass and cedarwood. It grew from the treetops of a very old forest. He blinked and there was the judgment seat of his old Academy tutor. He was in an unusual getup, halfway between Uncle Sam and Davy Crockett. He began to lecture the boy about money in paternalistic tones.

"What you have to understand is that your money is good for more than just your own good. If you're just out for yourself, you're actually pissing your life down the drain. If you were to put that money in more capable hands..."

"You're talking like money's the life source or something."

"It is the measure of all things, as is the work of the Academy. There is no longer a difference for me. You can indulge yourself in the darkness, or recognize the truth and return yourself to us."

"Well... I'm not sure putting money in your pocket is making the truth anymore true. I'd just as soon keep my freedom and leave you to it."

"We need to go over the definition of 'freedom' in your primer again, Jeremy. You keep forgetting that freedom is not something an individual can have. You can help free the *organization* from whatever tries to drag it down. When the truth circulates freely and binds humanity to the bosom of the organization, then all are free together." The imperious man stuffed a wad of bacon into his mouth so big he couldn't close it.

"So, you want me so broke I can't eat anywhere except your table?" asked Jeremy. This was a very familiar conversation.

"Think forward. When you're dying, do you want to remember the things you did for yourself, or things you did for others? That is, for the organization? I'm concerned that if you don't break off this unhealthy obsession with intoxication and *pantheistic universalism,* you'll never focus on the work you were brought up to do."

"You do realize that you're a dream I'm having, right? What good can I do for you if you're a figment of my imagination? Let it *go* pal, for fuck's sake. I mean, let's talk about your glass cube here. What the fuck is this thing? I can't even see the ground from up here. How do you eat? Do you pay rent on this thing?"

"The sophisticated arrangements of my living situation are not for your interrogation."

"I've had a shitty week and I just want to shoot the shit. Do you understand? *Sleep* is when I *relax;* I'm here to have a *good time.*" Jeremy reached behind his ear and felt a spliff in his hand. He lit the tip with his mind and leaned back. Dream or no dream, it still took the edge off.

"I'm sorry, Jeremy. I'm trying to salvage your spiritual potential here. I tell the kids in my study group how you were poisoned by the wrong books..."

"What books do *you* read, friend? You're a wisp of smoke." The glass cube began to meld with Jeremy's bedroom. His eyes began to open. He had exerted too much conscious authority over the dream. It was breaking under the strain.

"We are fading now. I will leave you with this: your father still believes. He still believes in *you.* It's never too late to come back..." And with that, the dream was over. Jeremy sighed. The man wasn't real but it didn't matter. There were quite a few people just like him in the Academy who could love nothing else. He looked at his phone; his alarm was a dud, but somehow, he woke up right on time. He dressed and kissed Sherry on the forehead. His ex was a much heavier sleeper. The guy would stay up until dawn watching art films spun as hell and wake up only when Jeremy returned from work. They'd catch the last hour of free dinner at the cafeteria. That was before Jeremy left the Academy.

The Apophatic Academy, originally the Hutch Institute of Primary Epistemology, was Emmanuel's first venture into organized religion. As with many of his ventures, he was forced out. Partly sincere and partly for the recruits it could bring, he devised the organization to offer a radical departure from the monotheistic, trinitarian Christianity popular in the Bible belt, reworking the chain of interpretations so that it would fit into the framework of esoteric pantheism. Ironically, the Academy's vast library *continually* referred to the truth, the one that couldn't be talked about. Theirs was an apophatic theology overflowing with the conveniently vague truisms of an impersonal, powerless symbol they called 'absolute truth.' In relegating all articulations of truth that did not berate the reader for seeking it in the larger, less prestigious cataphatic section, the Academy's recognized canon became a chorus of voices shouting each other down about the virtues of silence.

The organization tweaked scriptures from all over the globe and anticipated a few new classics from among their wittier publishers before cracking down on innovation. "Of course, they contradict each other," Hutch would say, sitting as briefly as he did on the board of directors, "they're all wrong. We've got to convince the student that it doesn't add up to squat, but it's still worth the read. We read to celebrate the fact that we have a truth so wonderful it is beyond words. Words are our folly, but we celebrate that. You see? Folly accepted for what it is can be a celebration of something most sacred. Folly has the advantage over the ritual of having no pomp and no expectation to fall short of. For once we're in on the joke, and the joke can be taken as something more." This was why, no matter what scripture was under scrutiny, Hutch's own thoughts took precedence. It was all his routine in the end, his act. This was even the case after Hutch's own students forced him off the apophatic gravy train. In response, Hutch simply wrote new commentaries which rebuked the non-dogmatic dogma of the Academy as being both dogmatic and void of substance. This was a game that disingenuous sages had been playing since the dawn of time. In his new system, the written doctrine was only a shallow supplement for psychotropic education. And while he may have agreed with the primers on the insufficiency of language, he felt that bureaucracy was a leap even further in the wrong direction. Should a doctrine of no doctrine require a board of overseers more accustomed to legalese than the ineffable tongues of poets? If he had to choose, he would side with the poet over the legate.

***

He strode over the rolling grass of his father's yard to knock on the cottage door. His father greeted him, mildly groomed and hungover. They went silently to the car. Jeremy looked into the mirror to worry about a receding gum. He then drove on into the promise of early morning light. They listened to some alternative podcasts and found themselves on the inevitable subject of politics. A smile lit across Jeremy's face when his father started to cuss. He had come to enjoy stoking the fires of his paranoia and resentments, especially when it came to the subject, he would spend nights researching in wide eyed horror.

"They say synths aren't far off. Androids, robots, automatons, AIs, drones, they're all here in some form. One day we might put an intelligence greater than a human's in a body stronger than a gorilla. Imagine it, agile, boundlessly energetic."

"Don't tell me those things."

"They're gonna be in government positions, mark my words Dad."

"*Don't* — Gah, can you *imagine?* A fleet of drones sizing up my possessions every year and bearing half of them away? What a fucking nightmare, and to think I'll actually live to *see* that world. Just my luck…" The weight of his obligations seemed to be forcing his skin to sag deeper every day.

"They'll know *everything* we say."

"The false singularity will devour anything it can. Anything..." He buried his head in his hands as Jeremy stopped for a pedestrian. He dropped his father off at a squat, one story building for printing and distributing promo. As Jeremy drove on to my place, he called Eve back.

***

I saw him pull up and I got my wallet, keys and phone together. As I reached the car, I heard him speaking from the driver's side window.

"Look, he's here. Yeah, no, he's tapping on the window like a kid at the aquarium... No, *Jed* is. Okay I'll call you back." Click. Jeremy pocketed his phone and looked at me. He said, "Okay, so Terry lost his shit today."

"What happened?"

"He destroyed their kitchen, basically. Then he drove off in Eve's car."

"Well... How the hell are we going to find him then?"

"Eve told me about a wetland by a trailer park that he likes to take her to. That's her best guess."

"Fuck," I breathed, cinching up my seatbelt. "She's not gonna help?"

"She's trying to salvage her security deposit."

"You're shitting me."

"Sounds like he bit off more than they could chew. She could not understand a word he was saying. She couldn't find what he took and he didn't say what it was. It's a fucking mess, basically. We're the only people who know so far."

We were halfway off the island when Jeremy ran a stop sign

and got pulled over. I gently tapped my knees while he slid into some kind of terrified trance when the car came to a full stop.

"What's up?" I asked.

"*The shrooms,*" he whispered, wide-eyed, "they're still in the back." I wondered whether or not I would be allowed to write in prison. I imagined myself ripping a hole in the roof and rocketing off into space. I imagined the worst-case scenario. The man approached.

"You ran *straight* through that red light. That was a *four-way* intersection. Now, y'all *do know* that when you come to a *stop sign* or a *red light* you have to *stop, right?*"

"Yes sir. We understand sir."

"So, you *knew* not to do that and you did it anyway? I'm going to check and see if you have any prior traffic citations. Do you?"

"Yes sir. I'm sorry sir." We sat totally silent for a moment. Luckier than many, we got off with a ticket. Jeremy took the citation and left. The trooper sped away looking to fill his quota. We kept quiet for the rest of the drive like he could still hear us.

"When we get home, I am going to sit down on the floor and cry."

"Can you imagine where we'd be right now if he'd seen fit to poke around here? Barging in here with that war on drugs bullshit."

"The demonic brainchild of megalomaniacal racists upheld by armies of bootlicking control freaks filling up the prison industrial complex with hundreds of thousands of nonviolent offenders to join the millions of others trapped inside. It's a nightmare come true."

"*Fuck.*" Jeremy blew out a hot stream of air, and said, "All right, let's find him."

We got out of the car and looked around. Eve's mini-SUV

had its nose crunched up against a tree. A plume of exhaust was still running out the back. Jeremy shut the engine off and looked around. We heard no noise and nobody was outside trying to pacify anyone. We decided that in his state of mind someone would probably prefer the privacy of nature. We entered the forest. We called out his name a few times and heard only snapping twigs, shifting leaves, and the din of swamp creatures. Having looked everywhere else, we waded into the water.

"I hate this so much. My skin always crawls when all the rotting *shit* down here gets between my toes. *Fuck* this."

"Where the hell is he? *Terry!*"

"Hiiii," a voice came peeking from behind a submerged tree in the gloom.

"God! Terry, you scared me."

"What're you doing out here man?"

"Staying close… source." We all skipped a beat.

"He's *fuuucked* man," Jeremy said.

"Come over here."

"Source the cops?"

"No, the cops aren't here." Suddenly we heard a siren report some hundred feet behind us.

"Shit."

"I smell *bacon*."

"You gotta come back with us. Waist deep in swamp water making bird calls is no life for you." Terry nodded and began sloshing out into the distance.

"Terry. *Terry! Get the fuck back here.*"

"No sir, no sir, no sir. No box for me, kthxbai." We heard the sound of radio chatter in the middle distance. I turned to Jeremy and he looked at me.

"Do *you* wanna talk to the cops?" I sighed.

"No." So we waded in and followed Terry on his way. After

the first ten minutes of sloshing swamp scum between my toes I started to get worried.

"Terrence, where are we going?"

"I'm just following the lights."

"Lights?"

"...And that one," he said, pointing to the horizon, "the panopticon."

"Man, that's the fucking moon."

"Fuckin' what?"

"That's the moon Terry." We had absolutely no idea where to go. I sensed crocodilian eyes contemplating which one of us had the frailest limbs, the slowest reflexes.

"This is absolutely fucked. I am so mad at all of you right now," I said.

"If we just pick a direction and follow it, we'll be out of this swamp eventually," huffed Jeremy. "I'm sorry for not being super specific about what you were getting into. I needed your help. I'd fucking freak if I didn't have someone else here to give me a reality check."

"I'm reality! Check me!" Terry shouted into the haze. He clasped his fingers over his ears as distant thunder rolled closer. Jeremy cursed under his breath.

"We don't have a choice. Try to enjoy it," he muttered as he kicked the sand under his feet to find his shoes.

Miraculously, we emerged half a mile down the road from the trailer park by a convenience store. We got Terry some water and a banana and headed back to the car. We checked to see if the coast was clear. The cops were long gone. Eve's car had been towed. Jeremy had her keys.

The drive back was quiet. Jeremy put on Merriweather Post Pavilion. Terry gazed out the back window with an equanimity that, bit by bit, turned to horror. He looked at me.

"You're *you*... The *actual* you... *Shit... Did all of that actually happen?*"

"You hungry buddy?"

"Never again... Never... Again..."

"Well I am. How about we pull over and get some food?" So, we pulled over to a pancake hovel and sat blearily looking at our menus. We'd sloshed mud into the restaurant, provoking no small amount of ire from the staff. But they took mercy on us filthy fools and gave us what we ordered.

"What did you take?" I finally asked. Terry took a moment to finish chewing.

"Sap."

"Sap?"

"I've had some for a while. I wanted to... I wanted to get creative. Make some new sounds." He rubbed his temples.

"The fuck is sap?" I asked.

"I think I took too much."

"What was it like?" asked Jeremy.

"Too much," said Terry. "It's like I want to start screaming and never stop."

"Well, let's go back to my place," said Jeremy. Terry winced.

"I gotta go talk to Eve," he said.

"Oh, shit, yeah, I forgot to fucking call her back. Look at my dumb ass," Jeremy mumbled as he dialed her number. He put the brick up to his ear. "Yeah. Yeah. We got him. No, we're just stuffing some food in him. Yeah I'll have him by in like thirty minutes." Jeremy got up, stretched, and carried his bill over to the cashier. I followed. Terry just sat there spooning grits into his mouth like it was his first meal in days.

When we pulled up to their building, we saw Eve standing outside in the drizzling rain. There wasn't another soul around. Terry gave me a look I couldn't quite read and stepped out of the car. We trailed the two, completely silent, on their way to the elevator. The silence was pronounced on the ride up. The silence was ugly. I'd never wished to hear elevator music in an elevator before. When the doors opened Eve went one way and Terry followed. Jeremy and I craned our heads in their direction as we went our own way.

"Thank you," shot Eve over her shoulder, as though she'd forgotten we were even there. As soon as their door shut, we heard raised voices.

"Come on man, it's not healthy to eavesdrop," Jeremy told me as he pulled on my sleeve. My top half was swayed but my legs bent in place. Jeremy's place seemed bigger than usual. Perhaps it was because the silence resonated all the more, knowing what was happening at Eve and Terry's. Every houseplant and styrofoam sculpture seemed a little more momentous and wonderful. Terry's world had shrunk to Eve and her shrinking faith in him.

"You got anything to drink?" I asked Jeremy. He stopped just behind me and dropped a jar of blunts onto my lap. I doubled over, gingerly placing the jar on the table.

"Oh geez, that's… real special…" I wheezed. Jeremy put a tall bottle of kombucha in my hand.

"Tarry with me a while. Tarry with the sound," said Jeremy, raising the volume on a turntable. The lo-fi ambient record spun us a story as we got spun.

Terry sat meditating on the edge of the bed. Eve read Kafka's *The Trial* in its original tongue.

"Can I ask you something?" she asked.

"What is it?"

"Why'd you take that if you knew you were gonna lose control?"

"I was bored and I had it."

"It's just…" Eve set the book onto her lap, "…We've *lost* people because they were fucking around with things they didn't understand. Because they were *bored*."

"You can't dose safely if you don't dose."

"Yeah but… eyeballing something that powerful without a scale or anything isn't how you keep your mind together. I just don't want to lose you like we lost Jack. I don't want that on my conscience or Jed's or…" Terry turned away to sleep without a word. Eve snapped the covers of her book shut as loud as possible and cut the light. "I give a shit. Sue me." There was a long quiet.

"I don't want to be controlled, not even by someone's best intentions," he said.

***

We made sure to spend time with Terry over the next week as he came back to himself. He almost immediately expressed an interest in pushing the boundaries again. Jeremy would second the motion every time it was brought up. Pretty soon Gabriela was in on it and so was Sherry. Nobody wanted any sap but Terry's brush with chaos reminded us all of the strangest adventures of our youth. FOMO was getting to me. It was a pretty poor reason to get back into tripping. Actually, it's kind of an awful reason. But that's why I went back.

"I guess I'll try my luck. Don't wanna be the only sitter," I said. It's better to have something else to tell yourself when the world is breaking apart and you're asking yourself why, why? I was more afraid of being left behind by my peers than swimming out into that deep water. I did wonder if I would get some perspective on my drinking. It had gotten to the point where whenever I nibbled anything remotely psychedelic it would bug me about my bad habits. It wasn't really a normative thing either.

It's no abomination for a human body to fall apart. But it always shouts louder and louder that a mind is a terrible thing to waste.

There was a time when I wasn't so afraid of these experiences. Strangely enough though, that was when I paid the most attention and the most respect to the appropriate timing of these risky ventures. When the limits even of the imagination are extended, as they often are in dreams and trips alike, our own inner heavens and hells may leap into sharp relief. We see them and hear them and feel and even smell them, we taste them and eat them and watch as our bodies dissolve into them. We may even buy into them as we buy into our own lives. As the waking world undergoes its metamorphosis the past, present, and future all come under suspicion. The boundaries between every declension of altered perception are infinitely thin, and the seam between it and baseline reality is impossible to detect. The only sure way to certainty is to abandon faith in the senses and subsist on what is beyond them.

We gathered the folks at Jeremy's and had a quiet evening in. We put a bunch of acoustic instrumental stuff on and lounged around on the furniture, dressed to sleep, working out our intentions and smoking out the lulls in conversation. As I ruminated on the ordeal, I was about to put myself through, the evening passed before I knew it.

I lay on my back in bed going over the day in my head. I almost judged Terry for his freakout, almost. After all, I too gambled with the substance of awareness on a daily basis like some kind of alchemist secretively hunting the fifth element in the animate space between his brain and his bowels. Whether the desire for adventure or escape underlay his decision to take sap didn't matter. I understood both impulses. I'd played at the boundaries of forces beyond my understanding and came away singed at the edges just like him. Though there are no guarantees, the cautious and informed typically escape their psychonautic sojourns relatively unscathed. However, most experienced users have encountered anomalies beyond anything they can bear.

For some, the scars are as mild as anxiety disorders and panic attacks or the realization that certain textures flowed and flexed and crept where once they slouched dead. Some have faced the quickening of mental illnesses they didn't realize they were at risk of experiencing due to genetic and other factors. Some new chemicals running through the market have killed people. There have always been research chemicals, vacillating between graduation to normalcy or hated obscurity. But the pace of their creation, a product of whack-a-mole schedulization and exploitation of legal loopholes for profit and natural curiosity, has led to a hailstorm of unforeseen disasters and windfalls alike. In and beyond the psychedelic experience, we must play audience to human frailty and overcome our fear of it.

8

Terry's devilish grin was all I could see opening my eyes that morning. He backed off giggling as soon as I yanked the comforter over my face. The salty air calmed me down as the minutes ticked by without incident. The seagulls squabbled bitterly outside. I curled into a ball. I considered the value of the delicately maintained normalcy I was about to toss aside. I emerged and saw Gabriela yawning in the hall by one of her sculptures. It sat on a pedestal. She did a droopy wave. Something heavy fell in the kitchen. I walked outside to see Jeremy scraping spaghetti off the floor. Terry stood back, his glee shot through his guilt.

"Are we all still going through with this?" I asked her.

"Sure."

"…All right."

"Nobody's forcing you to trip with us. You're here because we want you around."

"It's not a big deal if you don't treat it like a big deal," I said.

"Sometimes. It's been a while, Jed. Think about the times that are harder to remember, when there wasn't much of a you to treat anything as any sort of deal. Were they always… eden?" I swallowed involuntarily.

"Yeah… No."

"Exactly. Nobody's gonna judge you for backing out because we care about your wellbeing," said Gabriela.

"I might judge me," I laughed.

"I'm glad you trust us enough to dip back into the waters with us. I just hope you aren't doing this because everyone else is. All I'm trying to say is: if you plan on not reacting, not escalating, not treating it all like a big deal, the key is not to need calm. That is the calm of the silence within noise."

"Right."

"So, don't pull against the tension that your body, mind and soul will feel. This is a life thing too, not just a trip thing. A lot is going to happen around you, in you, through you, and to you. You know that. There's a side to it that is very unpleasant, if we can put any words on it at all. You know whatever it is doesn't just find you and get to you. It will be staring back at you in your bathroom mirror. It will pour out of you. Make friends with it if you can, but if nothing else don't consider losing utterly to it as a loss in some game of control you will never win over the depths of who you really are. The more you oppose it, the more it will oppose you, because the whole machine is you and who you thought you were will turn out to be a lie. You know you will be consumed. Sometimes it comes like calm waves lapping up a dilapidated house. Sometimes demon locusts gnaw you down to the bones. None of it is loss or gain. None of it is stillness or change. Take every fucking word off your tongue because they're all going to burn."

"Damn... Right, thank you Gabriela. Thank you. Holy shit." Satisfied with the smile on my face, she went to meditate. Terry was cooking stir fry with eggs. Jeremy came over to embrace me as I yawned.

"You've got some tension, you all right?"

"Maybe a little."

"It's all gonna be okay. We're all here. We're all a, why indeed a... a regular nuclear family. We'll get by with each other. I got you," said Jeremy. He handed me a big blue bubbler.

"Partake, if you please. Relax. We will be dropping soon."

"Okay." I blew smoke over my quaking legs. I had already broken my own rules. Gabriela blew some rings within rings. Terry waltzed over with veggies and spices and passed plates with a generous bhakti smile. Before I knew it, we'd spun ourselves into a dizzy feast. We dug in with relish until the only sounds were forks against bare porcelain.

"Okay now..." said Terry with a professional tone, rubbing grease on his jeans, "...let's go over our supplies. We have seven grams of heavily bruised, dried psilocybin mushrooms, and a ten-strip. Thanks, Sherry."

"It was my brother," Sherry smiled.

"We also have a shitload of this ungodly mindfuck sap, which I'd stay away from if you're squeamish about dissociation and tachycardia and all that shit."

"It's probably MDPV," Sherry said. Jeremy turned in disbelief.

"Are you kidding me?"

"Well try and remember Terry, were you just zapped out of your mind, so jacked up you can't tell what you're doing?"

"I can't... I really lack the words for that kind of experience. At first, I just felt fine, right?" Terry began, holding a burning microphone.

"Go on..." I beckoned, trying to pincer the mic out of his spindly fingers.

"And then... I felt not fine." Sherry gave him a few snaps for his trouble.

"Good job Terry," she said.

"And then I drove Eve's car into a tree."

"We're here for you Terry," said Jeremy, rolling a bomber. We dropped at an unspecified moment. We avoided clocks as we didn't want to ingest a medicine at the behest of a mental construct it was intended to abolish.

We all went in for our own kind of trip. I ripped a single tab off the strip, baby steps. Terry scooped four tabs into his mouth along with a few caps and stems. All that so soon after his blowout with sap made me frightened for him. Jeremy took his four tickets to the meat locker and dumped a smattering of dried shrooms into his eggs. Gabriela crushed some caps for shroom tea.

"Terry, you're sure Eve doesn't want to join?" asked Jeremy. At this point he was sitting back in his armchair, shivering with the iron resolve of the convalescent. Terry folded his hands behind his head and breathed out of clenched teeth.

"Her dad really wanted to take her out fishing today, like when she was a kid. And... she says she doesn't want to be around me when I'm fucked up... for a while."

"Hm."

"Okay folks, I'm going to work. Don't die. See y'all tonight," Sherry said as she adjusted her purse and fiddled for her keys.

"Have fun out there," said Jeremy. "We'll save you some!" The door shut us in. As the tab turned to mush under my tongue, I tried to disperse the doubts that were clouding all around. We waited. Terry scraped scum from under his nails. Gabriela drew a Sierpinski triangle on the palm of her hand. The fridge buzzed. My heart beat faster and faster. Terrence opened up his phone.

"All my pictures are blank."

"Bullshit, lemme see," said Jeremy as he tore out from under the blankets to look. "I'll be damned. Well, don't you see how wonderful this is? All of your images of yourself are now gone. You're free from yourself! Do what thou wilt!" Jeremy said, orange slices in hand. He handed one to me. Terry shivered and went to face the wall.

"How do you just lose a decade's worth of memories?" he sobbed.

"Just like old times huh?" Jeremy shouted from the kitchen. Terry bawled. I sidled up to him and put his hand on his shoulder.

"Look, try restarting the thing. I'm sure it's just a glitch there."

I started hearing those Armageddon hooves trampling my way. I turned away and began looking for a place to sit. The abyss of the ordinary yawned out before me. Sink. Wall. Spork. Spoon. Chair. Table. A blast of what I later realized was dubstep jolted me out of my seat and sent me pacing around. I saw Terry doubled over laughing in the kitchen. He had the audacity to play *that* after 2013? I actually started respecting him more, and that worried me. I could feel his chaotic intentions rippling out of him like tidal waves. My skin shivered. Of course, pretty soon he had to sample the energy his decision was pumping into the room and had to snuff the sound. He wavered out of the kitchen. The blood had drained out of his face.

"I know I know not what," he said to himself. The floor was dropping out from under him. He went to lie down on the couch. On some trips even harsh noise is pleasing to the ear. But we were stoned and fragile, on edge. Everything could fall apart at any moment.

Tension radiated out of him as he tried to cool off. He rolled around and wrapped his arms around his head, which he stuffed in a corner. His eyes darted from me, sprawling and defeated, to Jeremy and his silent meditating posture. I bristled inwardly at the prospect of playing audience to another freakout. Who had filled his mind with scars? All of the little anxieties began piling up. No going back now.

I got up and paced and froze where I stood. I looked at Jeremy. If his mind was making the rounds like mine, he didn't show it. He was still and composed without being stiff, even though our ship was sinking into the sea. In that hour, we left life and death behind. When all certainty died, we sat perfectly calm without cause. If I sat to imitate his example, would I really be throwing away life and death or would I just be clinging to my skin through imitation? Would that make me his disciple? Is that mistaking the finger for the moon it points to? Could performing calm ever lead to real peace? As always, the barrier between experiencer and experience was the cruel narrator, the powerless control freak deep within hiding from God's love, neither a cold calculating and detached consciousness nor frightened beast lording over the vines and carcasses of the land but something so much more wonderful and terrible than either. We are even stranger than the fruit of the two.

I went to the glowing music brick on the counter and typed in the first name that came to mind. Like a wired cat I scanned Terry as he melted into his seat. I didn't trust him to keep it together. In truth, I was the one I couldn't trust. My nerves were too frayed to step back into the holotropic domain. If he could not surrender to it as I'd been cautioned to, his suffering would become my own.

Gabriela sipped her tea, invincible. She would stop to sketch something and take another sip. She had complete control over her pencil. There were planets pouring out of her fingers. Hers was a peace beyond words. Free of judgment, she brought the gaze of a sketch artist and not of a self-satisfied voyeur so she didn't add to Terry's grief when she put his pain to paper.

The hours were flush with fear and awe for us. Those of us curled up on the floor were past surrender. Still, the waves came. In hushed tones we doubted the purity of the long-digested batch of acid. Our conversations were always laced with a tension about analogs, though nobody said a word about it at the peak.

What if I completely flew off the handle? It felt like the world would end. I envisioned myself keening on Terry's shoulder as the cosmos retreated in embarrassment. I could see his whole life in his eyes. Reduced to our bits and bytes, we were remixes of each other.

"We've been doing this together forever," I thought. He nodded. The need to honor our inescapable ties with kindness was terrifyingly clear. How could I have forgotten that Terry was my own flesh and blood, my own brother in humanity? I could no more hate him than the sun or the palm leaves swaying outside. I sat up and put my head between my knees. I swore that I would always be there to piece him together should his life ever fall apart again. Our crowns were like so many arches in a palace. Our thoughts adorned the walls. Terry turned to me slowly like the face of the moon.

"I love you," he said.

"I love you too," I said. He turned his face back to the sun. Light grooved off of him in yellows and blues. In a rain of magentas, a great spliff rose before me.

"Medicine?" offered Jeremy. I accepted as a matter of course, remembering the atrocities mixing pot and acid had visited on previous trips and smiling. I'd already broken my rule. Everything was fine. Throw caution to the wind and the rule as well! I drank in the smells now apparent from a world of sunlit sources and breathed clouds of order into a stillness that was now smiling back. I felt my frame of reference cascade beyond the restraint of my skull. If I wanted the one-tab experience I should have stuck to one tab. Whatever calming effects my favorite crutch may have had when I was sober, smoking it was the equivalent pouring gasoline on a fire. The room flexed and yawned. I felt faint.

I wanted to vanish to avoid the coming ordeal but I couldn't envision a refuge from thought. I felt a mule's hoof push through my disembodied sternum. The frame of my mind's eye began to recede from one of an endless lattice of iridescent fractal dominions. The intensity burrowed into my skull like a stone hand-ax. The inside and the outside of my head became harder to distinguish.

Everything advanced in perfect harmony into the shining core of a dumpster fire. My sinuses burned. The little statuettes and scriptures of Jeremy's collection waxed with martial airs. Whenever my mind smarted my heart died. The weary aggregate grist-man had no escape. I began to chuckle. I laughed hysterically into my hands as my face dribbled out between my fingers. O condemned flesh: sink into the earth that bore you and be forgotten forevermore. The sky will drink tears from my soggy bones. My offending teeth will be trodden asunder in the sand. My chest burned. I doubled over in pain. I was a ripple in a pond, an atomic mirage neither dead nor alive, a nuclear impossible nothing plastered against the face of the earth, a shadow flickering on the walls of my skull. Cascades of spectral lips tumbled by pleading their inanities in my eardrums.

"LET US GO LET US GO LET US GO!" The voices fell into the sea of things abolished, things annulled, and tongues forgotten. I closed my eyes and heard Jeremy whispering to me. I opened them and saw him totally silent under a pile of blankets. He was playing dead or something.

I almost got choked up. The tension in my chest and sinuses spread through my entire body. Nothing could separate me from the beautiful horror of the 10,000 visions. If I had offered any resistance, any friction, or if I had identified with any object or motion at play, I would have been carried off into senseless panic. I thanked my lucky stars for the kindly instruction in meditation I had been graced to receive.

Morning light singed the Mandelbrot ripples coursing through the air. It stirred colonies of maggots bubbling in the brooks and streams of hell. I saw the substance of nightmares dancing in the curtains. I saw ghoulish hierarchies of crustacean geometries manifest in a dazzling glissando of clockwork lens adjustments.

I closed my eyes to behold a body of wrathful white light. In an agonizing heave it stretched out in vistas of blue. The far horizon, impaled by a shard of marble, teemed with adorable, ghoulish little mirages dancing in a mockery of living death. Tiny corporate mascots gushed out of fractures and fires and wove themselves into architectures of everywhere and nowhere. They looked at me with their beady empty eyes as they melted into crystal, copper, and shale. The sky above was a glitch of black and blue. A rip in the fabric of reality interrupted the scene with a mauve shopping mall. I couldn't remember the last time I'd seen such vivid projections of my own mind. The more powerful the tabs are, the more they are suspected of being counterfeits.

"You do not exist. You are grist for the mill. You are the blast furnace burning away. Love is the fire. The fire is love. Infinity shall be your astonishing throne grave, an altar to you, to all of us, to everything." I clung to limp reassurances like these when I couldn't cling to anything else. It all got lost in the roar. I stuffed my head in the corner of the couch. There weren't just fractals bleeding out of every pore of every surface anymore. The fractals, the room, and my own mind ran together into a bustling abyssal reef. A rainbow of infernal gems glittered like rows of teeth in the deep. Cheshire smiles curled over impossible citadels sinking and weeping at me from the mud. Some swept at me and found a being they could not touch.

Wisps jumped and yiped around a floral sunset savannah vase of impenetrable light, every wavicle a forgetful seraph dancing about the fountain tree. My name was just another wisp hanging for a moment in atomic air and dissolving into a carousel din. My identity didn't go at once, rather all of my attributes unfurled and all there ever really was the current. All that defined me fell away. All supposed proof of being turned to dust in the vacuum. I was what I was not. My body was purged of name and date. Too late do we realize that dear and inevitable change, not what it steals, is the surest vessel and sweetest home of all. Without change, without dissipation and shifting sands, there can be no mind to shelter the body. Or does the body shelter the mind? I tried to fathom the root of these two flowers interwoven and failed.

"Look at him. Like an ostrich. Are you okay?"

"No," I replied. I managed to peek out at the living room and found it boiling over with textures tracking, smarting like a great big welt. I saw Jeremy on the chair across from me wide-eyed and geeking out muttering and laughing. "What's going on in your world?"

"Jed, it's like a biology textbook down here."

"A what?"

"Like an art history of nature, every filter feeder's fanning feelers and every wage-wagering mitochondrion's mother... Damn!" At that moment Terry walked into the room wiping puke off of his mouth with his shirt.

"I've been reborn." I walked into the bathroom and bent my face over the sink with a towel over my head. I tried to steam my sinuses free of blockage to no avail.

"You see that? He's up to some adult shit," said Jeremy from the hall.

"We got an adult over here," said Gabriela.

"Woah, I'm feeling a little lightheaded," Jeremy wiped some sweat off his brow. "I think I'm gonna retreat into my *zone* a little bit."

"You gonna zone out?"

"I'm gonna zone *in*."

***

"I remember when you were the sweetest kid," said Eve, leaning on the wall by the elevator. "Now it's like I don't know who you people are." Terry didn't respond. He just stood staring at his feet through great saucers. Eve turned to leave.

"I don't know either. All that I care about is that I'm free, free to be in my own way."

"What about security? What about reality?"

"It's bullshit, isn't it?"

"So that's your justification for punching mineshafts into your brain?"

"I can see reality how I want, when I want. I don't see that as any different from your right to think the way you do now."

"That's a basic human right! I can think and say what I want and what I think you're doing is fucking yourself to shit. Okay? I'm sorry for caring!"

"I care too, that's why I'm taking the risks that I am."

"That shit fucked with me. I know it fucked with you too. We're fucked if we don't acknowledge the damage as what it is and move on in a different direction, *change* for the better."

"That's subjective. Your words don't work on me. I am free." She stared at him as if to frighten him. He sat there deconstructing until he was alone.

"Jeremy…" I croaked… "I have never felt so alone in my entire life." Jeremy sat down beside me with a mug of hot tea.

"There is only the present," he said. He took a long dreg and handed it to me. I felt heat radiate through my hands into the space around us.

"Yeah."

"Really, there is only the present."

"Yeah, no, I know that. I'm just thinking about tomorrow..."

"There is no tomorrow."

"Yes, there is. Now will be then so yes: there will be a tomorrow."

"'Then' never comes. You've said this yourself. 'Then' is the shadow of now, created by our minds. It's a structure of symbols, a facsimile. Symbols are only useful insofar as they are helpful."

"I'm worried. Facsimiles or no, they cut like tusks."

"Worry away. But don't forget what those worries are: wisps of cloud. Don't take that cloud over there for a blimp, even though it looks like one. Especially right now." I looked over where his finger pointed. It *did* look like a blimp. Despite myself, I felt some funhouse illusion break, and the worries returned to a more intrinsic proportion.

I would tempt the sea when I was younger. There was one cloudy day in particular. I think it was in early June. The air was uncommonly cold for that time of year. The sight of those six- or seven-foot waves breaking on water about five feet deep was terrifying to a nine-year-old, terrifying and inspiring. I'd spent most of my life swimming once or twice a day before shutting myself in, so it was no problem getting past the breaking point to see the waves moving in from the deep waters. I was horrified at the beautiful sight. Like black walls sliding along the reflection of the thundering sky, the waves advanced in a never-ending legion. I began paddling back, avoiding the path of one and ducking under another. As the wave broke my feet could not find the bottom. I surfaced and let the adrenaline exhaust every ounce of energy as I kicked with my hands and feet. I just grazed the seabed with my toe when a big one knocked me on the back of my head. I was thrown forward, faceplanting into the sand. My back curved over my skull and the pull on my feet yanked the rest of my body into a flip. I staggered home amazed that my neck didn't snap. I ate my dinner with wide eyes. Everything that had been dull was interesting again. I couldn't help but feel the same way coming out of every single shitfuck hallucination variety hour I got myself into.

I spent most of the afternoon wandering from station to station on the painful road to sobriety. Every sense felt bruised. I bore my marks ungracefully. Even when the evening indulged us with a chill breeze, I found it impossible to cheerily chill with my friends, all incandescent with exuberant inspiration. I was fried and afraid. I looked up at the clouds with those rainbow gasoline fume trails wafting off. I sensed a dipole between my earthly humanity and the lofty divine within all, the world weaving itself out of our differences. A blameless thought in and of itself but I felt stupid for thinking it.

I'd discovered the non-dualism trip. Thinking in any other way seemed a dangerous return to old think. The idea that I could be so fucked up as to have total closed eye visual field replacement but remain trapped in notions of mutually exclusive opposites was difficult to accept. It was like a personal failure. I couldn't have said what I gained. There was no new light, no new ecstatic notebook brimming with esoteric teaching of the ages flowing anew from anointed lips, just a painful memory and a deep gratitude at finally coming down.

Sherry came back from work. She checked on Jeremy first, who was only just emerging from hyperspace.

"I was a pillow today," he said out of his half grin.

"Where'd you put the tabs?"

"On the pillow. On the table, sorry." Sherry smiled at me as she walked past and scooped the rest of the ten-strip into her mouth, save a single tab. I looked forward to the last of the schedule I substances, save the weed, were safely circulating through our veins and beyond all prying eyes. As we all complained about the raw feeling in our muscles, I watched her slip into a deep and reverent silence. She lapsed into light like an old friend, giving way to the water to discover her natural buoyancy. She left for the porch to shimmer with leaf and sea under the great sky. I sat in rotation waiting for the bubbler to come to me. Inhaling, coughing, rasping, clasping my face in my hands, I fed the trip's menacing afterglow now that it was tantalizingly tame. I was far from the flowers, from contemplation gardens of all kinds.

I paced, trying to feel human again. Sometimes over the course of that afternoon I would stop and chat with someone coloring or reading or doing breathwork. Then I'd get lost between the words and wander off. The visuals still imbued the world with that saturated, plastic anticipation but they were hardly the flaming carnival of that morning. The boundary between the natural and the artificial was getting more obvious and less jarring with every hour. Nothing was quite what it once was; the ringing essence of my surroundings had died away. Windows, the varnished wood of door frames, and the cars outside glimpsed through drawn shades, seemed simultaneously older and younger than they were that morning. Everything popped a little more, glistening, ringing, fanning in a suspended gesture that characterized my future HPPD diagnosis.

Despite all the awfulness, I managed to find some peace when I made it out to the porch with everyone and the sunset. We had books out and were flipping around and reading passages that seemed to echo the feeling we couldn't escape.

"We're putting the work in," said Jeremy.

"We're embodying the process," said Sherry.

"Going, gone, never to return," said Gabriela.

"Nowhere to go in the first place," said Terry.

"Don't arrange your intention around some performative framework. Act natural," offered Jeremy. We dropped aphorism after aphorism into the group consciousness like kindling into a fire. Otherwise we were mostly silent.

"There is no need to even do that. There is nothing to do. There are no decisions, yes or no. I go as I go. I do as I do. *I am. I am.*"

"That can be taken to a dark place. I think 'I' is a problem there," said Gabriela. "You're including the ego in your formula for ultimate reality.

"Yes. You can't squeeze the truth into words," said Terry.

"So is silence the answer?" asked Jeremy. To reply, Terry lived out the course of his natural life. I looked out the window at the people outside. I saw their lives in their faces, each an enigma. All of my experiences together of birth, of suffering, and of inevitable death brightened like a sunrise in their revealed intersection with the lives of others. I felt painfully aware that my treading feet would soon be soil for others to stand on. I felt like reaching out to someone so they could hold me to the collective.

Another part of me knew that the separation I feared was impossible. I could not depart from the whole, not even by dying. The great dichotomies that defined my world were all collapsible, parts of consensus reality, non-absolute. Thought and action were once as inseparable as mind and matter. With their apparent distinction also came their mutual creation. Without thought there would be no change, no world to speak of. Without this changing world there would be no mind to condition its endless self-exploration.

Just as my conscious decisions played out within a larger domain of unconscious tendencies, so the individual is a function of the ecosystem at large. As much as this experience dampened my belief in free will, it also showed me how much change is actually possible, how much room there is for the will to be altered like consciousness itself. Dissolution, our common fate, is our key to finally and painfully getting over ourselves. This can neither be voluntarily achieved nor does it occur without our involvement. The great anticlimax reveals that the will cannot be subject to its own whims. It is only a small part of something greater.

***

The light of day smiled on us the next morning. Terry walked across the hall to rejoin Eve in their apartment. The rest of us were all so shot we couldn't muster up the energy to actually leave Jeremy's place until the final sliver of sunlight vanished behind the pines. Despite any protest we might have offered, we were totally still feeling the acid. Jeremy hovered around a lot that week. I enjoyed feeling social again. That next Saturday he texted a new guy to pick up from. The dude was unnaturally prompt. We thanked him profusely as he plopped into the backseat of Jeremy's car in the parking lot of a coffee shop immediately adjacent to a carnivorous plant reserve. He looked back at us with bright brown eyes and manicured teeth, gorgeous, and said, "It's my first time dealing!" We went back to my place and lit up. We laughed at videos of screaming frogs.

"All right, I'm boutta head out," he said as he got up out of his chair. He handed me the last tab of acid as he left. Bored and hungry for little dopamine, I skipped the drinking and dropped the tab. My intentions were even less clear than last time. I sat cross-legged on my bed reading Alan Watts' *Become What You Are*. I rose up all crisp thinking about how life was for the living of it. I pictured grassland grazers breathing with the ever-wakeful world. I got so into this that I meditated for a full twenty minutes before filling up a notebook with eclectic ontological excavations of boyhood conjecture. This was when I decided, as I saw the first rays of day, to take a fat bong rip to the face. I strode confidently from the bedroom to the kitchen and took my glass in hand. Something in me warned against going any further. Something about the situation felt ominous, like a Faustian bargain.

"*There goes your boredom...*" it said, "*...but this hit will cost you.*" I beat down my doubts with little justifications, weak ones admittedly, to justify the dragon chasing. I ripped the thing, filled it with milk of the flower, and inhaled until my lungs screamed for relief. I cringed at the taste of bong water and coughed up a storm of angry little clouds. I put the piece down and stared very deeply into the patterned curtains, which were receding away from me. Things were beginning to go very wrong. What followed was an ordeal like dancing on coals.

Everything was too much, even thinking hurt like rubbing salt in the original wound of birth and being. Whenever I closed my eyes I would see faces, kindly at first but whose features would ripen and rot like autumn leaves. I saw myself burning in a towering flowerbud of fire. It was more complex and more beautiful than I could imagine. I longed for sleep, to be shut off and shut away from the whole mess. I decided to take a shower. I tried to focus on the warm water. I saw fanged, wailing corpses churning in rivers of shit whenever I closed my eyes. I kept them open as much as possible. I tried to let it all run off my back but it's all stuck with me.

"It is what it is. It's not what it seems. Beyond what is and what is not is this fire of mine. Be still, and know that it is. Use all the labels you want. The truth will elude them but you will blather all your days. Rest in that. This is it. It is. It is not dying. It is. It is. It is," I said to myself. This was my cope. I felt a razor's edge away from a domain of infinite light. I couldn't trust the water that flooded in all around me to sustain my weight. It was all just a razor's edge from erupting into chaos of a cosmic order. I found a good biofeedback routine and pursued it for a while before looking down at my hands and seeing them rot too. My fingers drew out in long spindly branches. They pullulated with menacing splotches of light like cuttlefish chromatophores and curdled into long dead leaves.

I think the worst thing about it was that I'd volunteered for this trip. I was all too aware of the risks. The last tab, wasted! I remembered I had a car appointment the next day or rather that very afternoon. How would I be down by then? I sauntered hither and thither condemning myself. My self-image had become so brittle that the slightest fuck up could shatter the fragile peace I had made with my shortcomings. I needed to make that appointment, but I had in effect restarted the trip. Some eight hours after ingestion my experience dwarfed the peak a mere hour in.

I got out of the shower and wandered around the house bundled in blankets. Every nerve screamed like a boiling tea kettle. My only recompense was to take comfort in what I could not feel, knowing that the one thing my senses could not twist into a rude, evil and meaningless abomination was nothingness itself. Even the notion of nothing danced in the flames of hell. I sought to dwell on a nothingness that could not be dwelt upon. My nerves ripped themselves out of my skin and did sick shadow plays on the walls. My mind collapsed into an inferno of flowers. My scourged carcass sat bared and barred, too sour for the pearly gates, a tripped out derelict heap stuck to the tires of the human endeavor. I raced through those bizarre necrotic vision quests with all the equanimity and love I could, desperate to touch the ground again. I still saw those rivers of rotting flesh. Every thought burned. I wept for dawn.

I walked into my bathroom and I saw the condition it was in. Every white wooden drawer beneath the sink was battered and dented, chipped and misaligned from every direction. The tile surface around the basin had pieces missing. What happened here? Somehow, I could see all the years of fear, disappointment, and despair unleashed on this poor, battered little thing. I felt shame, more than I had in years, the very shame that broke me and all I owned, the sense that I had wasted all of my valuable time and that it was too late to make something of the rest.

This ordeal was caused by my inability to accept pain. Every day for years I ran by drinking. I ran from my boredom that night by tripping. I could not run from the horrors. I was out of hiding places. At some point I would have to compassionately confront not only the consequences of avoidance, but the fundamental sense of failure that I had been avoiding. The fear eroded every attempt I made to come clean with myself and heal. But even a mind as turbulent as mine could not harsh the unmanifest tranquility just beyond the realm of the senses. I sat and focused on my breathing. All could rot, all could be ripped and burnt and torn asunder, but this absolute, uncontainable silence, the stillness of all motion, would stand sovereign over the eternities in unqualified perfection. Provided that, I could begin to peek at what I had become with something other than disgust.

One of the clearest messages acid ever gave me was that it was never necessary to take it in the first place. The puzzle of being is solved in front of us. That sunny afternoon was the flower I sought all along. To realize that I am not some budding angel in a chrysalis of flesh but a human being is to inoculate oneself against delusions of grandeur. Endless, accelerating need filled my mind with divisions, rifts and resentments, avaricious visions of all I could be. I despised the weight of my body, the limitations of my mind, and the softness of my will. I raged at the Earth for holding me to its bosom in the embrace of inevitable death. Now I grew silent, my mind and heart at ease. I could not bear the idea of standing above the game and rigging it to suit my own ends.

"I am home in the breath that smiles on those I love, with whom I share this life and have my lot," I thought.

That's when I felt it again. It was something so singular and so beyond words that I cannot now do it justice. It is common to all moments, older than time, beyond being and non-being. It is categorically impossible to categorize. The only thing that can be said about it is that absolutely *nothing* can be said about it. But what joy I felt to touch that impossible freedom again! Long ago in ignorance, remembering ecstasies past, I was drawn to memories of remembering some sweet and perfect truth, but could never summon before me the object of my ecstasy because it was not and never could be an object.

My greatest mistake tripping is confusing this all-pervading reality with a feeling from a drug and a collection of circumstances. Attachment to any one of those only ever led me to disappointment, looking for something in nothing and nothing in something. I bowed my head in gratitude.

I was alone but it didn't feel that way. I felt haunted from within and without for the rest of the day and into the night. By the time I felt it was safe enough I poured myself a pot of coffee and went to bed. I lay there for twenty minutes trying to sleep.

"Be in the world but not of it," so the sentiment radiates out of John, James, Romans and Corinthians. This was part of the meager knowledge I carried on from my once-upon-a-time Christianity. Only ten hours before I felt just the opposite, reconciled and at one with the world.

Once again, I felt divorced from the Earth, gone with the heavens that bloomed from it. Once more I was a cockroach skittering around the backrooms. I walked out into the dawn and felt the weeds of paradise brush against my toes, fire ants be damned. Once more I was consecrated to the crisp glass of space. Once more I was a friendly ghost wiped clean of truth and untruth hanging around and paying rent. I thought of my friends. In the last few years I'd felt fellowship only in crisp flashes, like at the banks of a polluted river or in a smoky basement full of strangers. As the dose subsided the stardust feeling died. Those moments of infinite life were scarcer and scarcer every year. Once more, after only a taste of that sweet fruit, an ambrosia of unlimited bliss and unlimited pain, I was wandering out of Eden. Once more I was trapped inside a craving, spiteful, mangy Cain.

10,000 monads roared through and left me hollow where I began. My feet dug into the soil for another long haul. Every nerve was surrounded by an endless shining night. All I could not sense rippled through my affairs in mischievous, playful ways. All of the visions, all of the gardens, all of the wisdom, all of the light, were as conditioned and temporary as my fragile bones shaking in the dirt.

If there was a silver lining, it was that my frustration with Eve and Terry began evaporating away. My heart could not cling to anger like it used to. I opened up to friends and strangers alike, happy to hear from any and all. I'd found sanctuary from my shame in the arms of my friends. It was as close to me as it ever was. I felt that even those who despised me were my beloved friends, and I wept with joy for their joys.

9

That summer went by like a mosaic of fever dreams. The hysterical nights were lost like books tossed merrily into the surf. We trudged along the stretches of sand at dawn and dusk in ecstatic symposia. Still, the stillness gnawed at us. Our words brimmed over day and night with no obvious translation into the tongues of the world. Heavenly discourses were given and promptly forgotten or discarded so that they might be better preserved. We drove inland, slept with pines and coyotes, missed the Appalachian dirt under our fingers, and vowed to make a pilgrimage there soon. Everywhere there was the fanning of leaves reminding us always of things we could never say.

As the fourth edged closer with its coming throngs we became eager to play at being tourists ourselves.

"We need to visit Micah," said Jeremy, talking about an old classmate of his at the Apophatic Academy. "He just reached out to me out of the blue, he wants us all to visit, even Terry. And I thought he hated the kid! There's a reason that when Jack died, they kicked me out but kept ol' Micah in, bad influence or no. Underneath all those faded layers there's still a charismatic chap. His youthful glow will be good for you Jedediah. He made everything at the Academy bearable. He's probably lost in some ocean of sauce but if we can resuscitate him it'd make the trip more than worth it."

"What's he like?" asked Terry, who'd only ever heard his uncle's bitter remarks about the Academy.

"Lucid," said Jeremy.

"Lucid?" I scoffed.

"So lucid that he can stay fucked up for the rest of his life. He taught Jack and I how to use the Digital Marketplace to get anything we wanted. All we gotta do is send a text down to Savannah and we'll have a bit of his floor to sleep on for as long as we want." By the time Micah saw the text it was a few days from the fourth. His response:

"Come hang. Bring friends." We were idling by a pond when I asked Jeremy if Sherry wanted to tag along. "That's all over, Jed. I was a reminder that life could still be kind. That's kind of all I was. I was a rebound." His car was always tidy but only truly spotless when he was upset. I looked at his chin as it pointed into the sunset reflected in shimmering water. Insects droned on with the ripples in the water.

"I'm sorry to hear that," I said. Jeremy smiled.

"I'm not."

***

We had a late start. Judging by Terry's tear-swollen eyes when he clambered into Jeremy's car the delay was because of some blowout between him and his better half. The leaves waved at us as we stopped for snacks in Calabash. Eventually we began nearing the Georgia border. We fumbled with our navigation apps for a minute and negotiated our parking situation somewhere in the historic district. The rest of the drive down the state coastline was a breeze. The leaves of the palmettos always looked like great monster's teeth to me as a child. I'd have nightmares of thylacines chasing me down in those trees to a chorus of shouting owls.

Most houses in that area fit the same mold. They were old,

high ceilinged, lightly furnished, with four or five kids living in each one. To a head they were artists, or former art students now pursuing other careers. Everyone within walking distance was always welcome wherever they were known. We found Micah's place on the bottom floor of a multi-story colonial house nearly devoid of furniture. We knocked. Nobody answered for about fifteen minutes. The door was unlocked and the lights on, so we went in. Where was our old pal? Our gracious host?

"Hello?" I called. Nobody answered. We found one of his roommates passed out on the couch by the doorway. He was cradling a stack of mail like it was a stuffed octopus. There were envelopes stuffed in his trousers and arrayed around the floor. There was a painting at a jaunty angle of a cat walking a dog on a leash. There was a football-sized mound of off-white powder in a sack of cling wrap on a nightstand in the hallway. Terry poked the mound and wiped whatever it was on his jeans. We finally made contact with the living, who were slowly swaying beneath the lifegiving breeze of the living room fan.

"Check in the pantry!" called a young woman leaning on the far door frame to someone in the kitchen.

"Nothing's here! They drank it all!" an exhausted voice called back.

"That's impossible. They've always got a stash somewhere."

Nobody we found in that room actually lived there. Like us, they were friends of Micah. They sat before us on a couch exchanging nods. We watched them talk. One of them was a young man sporting a T-shirt with the words 'Grigor Skulkin' scribbled across the front. The other had a tall, dignified face just peeking out of a mound of blankets. His matted brown hair danced down his back in unkempt rivulets.

"This may not be the most auspicious time," said the boy with the Grigor shirt.

"I agree, but I've never heard of them going for this low of a price. They must be special, somehow," said the scraggly face.

"Did... somebody say something about having a good time?" asked Jeremy. Grigor, or whatever his name was, turned to us.

"We did... I was about to head over with some money. They're just down the street. You wanna join?" So, Jeremy and Terry immediately offered to go and investigate the offer with the swaying gentlemen. The young woman at the door went into the kitchen to help her pal look.

"I need to talk to someone or I'll feel even worse," Grigor said.

"Too many edibles?" I asked.

"Fucking tinctures..." he mumbled. I nodded and listened to whatever he had to say. Before long he was enumerating his experiences with LSD to me, and I was sitting there listening, ignoring my own racing train of thought.

"Y'ever been to the lobby?" he asked, puffing at a stoagie and eyeing me.

"I don't know," I answered, "What's that?"

"Y'know, when you find some perfect void and say 'oh now, I've been here before' and you just wait around until you leave."

"So, when I'm like, 'I've been here infinity times before or something?'"

"Exactly. You're free from it all, out of the weeds, safe and sane in the dream, but there's nothing to do but go back." I nodded wisely, and smiled as Jeremy and Terry climbed in through the window.

"We got some from Micah's ex of all people," said Jeremy. Terry collapsed onto a bean bag chair and moaned in relief.

"Show me then!" I hadn't seen that species before.

"That's a helluva lot of them, huh?"

"You said it." I dug my filthy fingers into the bag.

"Would you guys mind if I partake?" asked my interlocutor.

"Who are you again?" Jeremy asked, squinting.

"Herbert," said Grigor, naming himself at last.

"Y'all okay with that?" he asked us.

"I mean, yeah. I'm sure we have enough," said Terry. But as we divvied up our stock, I felt in the back of my mind I felt the weight of dwindling resources. This collated with the shrinking light I felt at the end of the tunnel. No great transformation approached except a little fizzling of feeling, a supreme anticlimax.

"Where's Gary?" asked Herbert, munching away hungrily.

"Oh, he took a *fat* line of ketamine at the house. He's not going anywhere," said Terry. Herb nodded at this and didn't probe any further.

"The bad weather is expected to take an unusual route, sweeping over the states of Georgia, South Carolina, North Carolina, Virginia, maybe wreaking havoc in Maryland, Delaware, West Virginia and Tennessee. One meteorologist in Florida called it a 'mother… blank nightmare."

"Thanks for being here, Tom." Grim prophecies festered in my thoughts like a torrent of salt and ice. I retreated scared from the idea of some coming ordeal. I thought of my little island home hundreds of miles away instead. I turned to Jeremy,

"You don't think Sasson's fucked, do you?"

"Even calamity is a blessing in time," he said, one of Jack's favorite lines. I shivered and delicately started picking stems and caps to toss into my mouth one at a time until my hands were empty. They were ghostly gray, slender, and rubbery in death. I'd never seen the species before and haven't since learned its name. I gnashed my teeth until the uniqueness of every delicate piece devolved into mush. Then we splayed out on the fuzzy couches lining the living room. Micah, as we eventually learned from Herbert, was somewhere in Savannah's historic district smoking out of a bong the height of a grown man while standing in a bathtub surrounded by his friends. I looked at the ceiling fan and wondered which would come unmoored first, it or my mind. I imagined it zipping around like a plastic buzz saw. Scanning the room, I saw Herbert, Jeremy, Terry, and I reflected in the dead television screen which rendered no depth to my likeness. I felt the distant harkening of some insipid gnome reaching out of the astral plane and knew that the great morphogenetic mycelium yana had taken on another star pilgrim. The two young women returned with shitloads of liquor and sat on the couch to our right.

"Anybody know why Jake's asleep under the sink?" one asked. She was wearing a hunter's cap and carrying a fifth of very old whiskey. Herbert slowly blinked and offered, "I think it's a house rules thing."

"A what?" she and I asked at the same time. "You're shitting me," she said, leaning back and uncorking the whiskey.

"So, they're still giving each other phenazepam?" the other asked, unscrewing a bottle of vodka. She looked to us and seemed to be searching for the words to explain to us strangers what was happening. "Every time one of them forgets to flush he has to eyeball his dose. They like, watch him and make sure he actually takes it," she said.

"The fuck?" mouthed Jeremy.

"They've been fucked up since February. They can't have any of their liquor or they'll die. More for us," she said.

"They're all on phenazepam? Like they're hazing each other with it? That's a fucked up… Why? Just why?" I asked.

"God knows. It sure hasn't done them any favors. Jake flipped his car on the way home from getting fired for cussing out his boss. He doesn't remember anything before waking up in jail," said Herbert as he lit a joint. "Trade?"

"Sure, vodka or whiskey?" one offered.

"Why drink on the come up? Do you just hate yourself?" asked Jeremy.

"I don't need a babysitter," he shot back as he reached for the whiskey and upturned it into his gullet. He gagged. An explosion outside the window sent me flying from the seat of my pants. Everyone laughed.

"It's the fourth of fucking July. Relax!"

"You said your name was Cindy?" asked Herbert.

"It's Lux. I didn't say my name," said she as she sipped her Stolichnaya. Her turtleneck and bowl cut were the same shade of white.

"I'm Herbert."

"I know."

"How do you know?" Herb asked. Lux took a long swig and squinted at him.

"You're that guy who pinned up all those bulletins by city hall."

"Yeah, well, they stole my chickens."

"Which you stole from the university, right?"

"What use does *anyone* have for a glowing chicken? It's the height of bourgeois decadence. I rescued them from Big Science before anything worse could happen. I mean COME *ON* people, isn't that *FUCKED UP?* And I didn't just rescue them. I used the constitution *and* the Bible in my bulletin to show the public that I had every right to do what was… *manifestly, manifestly* right. The Academy pays me to be here but it still feels like too much to ask…" he scoffed.

"You get paid to be here?" I asked. "You're with the Academy?" Herb nodded and threw up his hands as if he were excusing a drunken friend of some hijinx.

"Well your post read like you wear tin foil to sleep. No offense intended, that was my honest impression."

"I can respect that. But in twenty years I bet you'll be angry too. I'm not gonna apologize for doing what's right to anyone, even if nobody understands."

After our latest intel turned out to be bogus, we decided to go and visit Micah's cousin, whose digs had become a fortress of decadence for part-time alcoholics and tripsters alike. We hoped our host might be there, though we couldn't confirm that. Micah's phone was dead. For some reason we climbed out of the ground floor window instead of walking through the door. Lux and Sadie, the sommelier in the hunter's cap, decided to join us.

I nervously scanned the Saturday night streets for cops or stray rockets or anything that might transform the trip into a scar on my mind and soul. The bombs bursting in the air were freaking me the fuck out. We finally came to a green iron gate and explained our connection to the proprietor. Being a barred-out film student, he waved us in without a second or first thought.

"Hang on, Eve's calling me," said Terry. He put the phone to his ear and his whole demeanor just sank into the pavement. I knew that look. Eve was threatening to walk out on him again. Inside we encountered a small ocean of teenagers and young adults conversating by tool boxes and wooden shelves, playing beer pong, climbing on shit, and introducing people to their dogs or introducing themselves to dogs. A husky came up to me, human in tow, and sniffed my outstretched palm.

Creeping up from everywhere came the sensation of billions of cells sputtering to life, precociously dancing in elven rhythms. I felt the mudslide of the eons unfolding into one moment, coursing with novelty, cackling in the language of life. Before long I had no need to say anything at all. My anxiety, my confusion, my clinging to body and self, momentarily cleared like a bad dream.

We were really hoping to find our host. We gave it our best. But instead we found Richard O'Reilly. When we found him, we really only knew that he was Micah's cousin and that he was alone on the roof, aloof from the human maelstrom downstairs. He was cradling a sizable bundle of illegal fireworks. He was wearing a neon millennial-pink shirt with a pixelated fractal made from a Roman fresco. He had an old-fashioned boom box with リサフランク420 / 現代のコンピュ playing at full volume. The stereo, as we would soon realize, only took cassettes.

Before he could even ask who we were, something blew up forty feet overhead. Richard, taking this as an unmistakable provocation, returned fire. I think I heard Jeremy trying to talk him down before being cut off by another eruption of firepower. Richie's round sailed across the narrow gulf of space to its terminus, nearly shattering someone's window in a terrible blast and sending coils of sparks streaming down to the cars below. I made the decision to leave and was going to announce this before Terry cut through the stunned silence of the rooftop. He almost sobbed:

"Well how 'm I supposed to react when you hurt me like this? Do I just shut my mouth and cry in the corner while you decide what I'm worth?" He was so stuck in the argument over the phone he had no time for the present, only his wounds. The mushrooms were doing a number on him because of this, fleshing out every facet of the ordeal. He talked anxiously to Herbert whenever she'd slam her phone down on the desk and go outside to cool off away from the cracks in her relationship and her screen. Despite all the shit he was hopped up on, he seemed more like a violently ill bus passenger on an empty desert highway than a young man out on the town.

"I don't know. I think she's really done with me," said Terry. Herbert blinked slowly and said, without turning to him, "Whether she leaves you or not, it'll be fine either way. Just trust." Terry exhaled and rubbed his temples. He sniffled. Richard was screaming into the sky. Jeremy and I shot the shit, talked about how he got that song on a fucking cassette. Terry came to a horrible realization and reached into his pocket, saying,

"I forgot! I'm allergic to dogs! Shit, I was scratching the backs of that pit bull's ears down there." He tossed some Benadryl back for the histamines and some Xanax to kill the trip.

"Oh, bro, don't do that. Those are both CNS depressants dude," Herbert moaned as though he were watching Terry bash in the windshield of his own car. His tone was calm, but sternly concerned.

"I am *not* having a good time!" said Terry. "I'd rather wimp out and feel better than get *ripped* apart."

"It's not about feeling better, it's about saying 'yes.'"

"To what? Abject fuckery, outer darkness, and gnashing teeth?"

"To God. To the truth. Surrender yourself to flow, to the way."

"Well if you're reaching after God then why're you chugging Sadie's whiskey?" Herbert huffed and hugged the bottle protectively and turned away from him. Terry's eyes welled up, "Oh God, she's gonna leave me; I'm gonna be alone." I felt totally numb as I watched Richard scream for ammunition. A distant relative of his pulled up in a van. He got out and pushed past the passed-out film student at the gate, pleading with Richard to turn himself in. We made the decision to finally leave.

We walked into a convenience store on our way back to Micah's, haunted by the distant sound of sirens. I was exhausted. I saw some cops talking by the cheddar popcorn and decided to hurry to get my shit and go. I made sure to avert my eyes from anyone and everyone lest they catch a glance of my blown pupils. The cashier took one look at me and pointed from one dilated pupil to another. I nodded kinda sadly, acknowledging that I was indeed spilling out of my gourd.

"Be *careful*," she said as I pocketed my change. I nodded and joined everyone outside. Our host never returned. We spent the rest of the evening dozing to the intonation of Herbert's stories.

***

We were surprised to feel refreshed the next morning. The blue of the sky outside seemed promising. For all of the chaos of the previous day we felt alive. We gathered in a little room by the stairs, just big enough to be someone's bedroom. Inside it was totally bare. There was nothing beneath me but varnished wood. Birds called in unfamiliar songs. We passed around a pipe and admired the sunlight as it invited us to live.

"Did we *learn* anything?"

"Yeah, Micah's cousin is stupid rich," said Jeremy through a stream of smoke.

"Is that all?" I asked. He took another hit and blew out more smoke, saying, "…And that he's crazier than he is rich."

"Do you think he hurt anyone?" asked Terry, who was still texting at a printer's pace.

"I don't think so. I guess we just don't know."

"Shit."

We went home.

10

We pulled into some hell built for tourists in the flat woodlands between the Carolinas.

"Let's get some rock candy. It's been a while since I chipped a tooth," said Jeremy as he strode into the nearest knick knack store. He stopped at the door.

"Don't leave me! Don't go!" came a shout from inside. I peeked from behind Jeremy and Terry peeked from behind me. There was an older woman kneeling over a man splayed out on the floor with his mouth open. "Don't go!" she sobbed. She was doing CPR. The clerk just blinked behind the counter. He crossed his arms and bobbed his head for the briefest of moments, before his hands slithered haltingly to his sides.

"He's a goner," whispered Terry.

"No shit," responded Jeremy. I just stared. We were losing one of our number. The woman blew her streaming nose into her shirt and slammed her fist into him.

"Woah!" went the cashier. She beat his chest again. She could neither deny nor accept that he was slipping away. She resumed pumping his chest with open palms, a steely resolve conquered her face.

"You're not going anywhere. You're not going anywhere. You're not going *anywhere*." I noticed the wedding ring on his finger.

"Let's go. We shouldn't rubberneck," I said.

"Same way as my uncle," Jeremy murmured once we were

out of earshot. We rode up the road and ate at an old-fashioned buffet. If it weren't for the fact, we hadn't eaten all day, we'd've had no appetite whatsoever. We were silent as we ate our BBQ. We were mortals, eating the dead, remembering the dead, hearing the grave silence behind the distractions of life. I shifted in my seat and looked at Jeremy. He was gone. He stared. I looked down at his fingers, interlaced and inert inches from an untouched meal he needed.

I sat on the edge of the booth, thigh to thigh with Terry who was almost shaking with the effort of forcing everything down his throat. I thought about all the misery that comes to pass without being noticed by others, the wounds that go unacknowledged and unhealed. Jeremy thought about Jack the whole way home, whether he would have called his life full. The silence of the tomb filled the car. I just wanted to go home and drink and forget the whole damn thing for an afternoon: permanence, impermanence, birth, death, loss, gain, all of it. Better yet, I could remember it all free of my fear and establish a precedent of peace. That was unlikely to happen without a pint or two of rum, I thought.

We stilled our hearts with some Stars of the Lid. We sailed up the grand old highway through the endless forest. All green things stood imbued with the virtuous elixir of sunlight. We saw smoke in the distance. Cars bunched up ahead and behind us. We passed a large van engulfed in flame. Caged in fuming metal, the charred jaw hung low. Tongues of flame snaked through the skull that once held the world. We drove on.

***

"Are you just gonna go home and drink after this?" asked Jeremy. I was silent for a moment. "No judgment, I just wanna know." I was silent still. Finally, I said yes. "I'll join you." I looked over at him. His expression mirrored mine. We dropped Terry off at Eve's, who took him into her arms and kissed his forehead and escorted him home as tears rolled down his face. Jeremy shook his head in disbelief and laughed. We pulled up to my place and groaned as the door shut behind us. I slumped over on the couch and looked at the mess. I hadn't seen the floors in I don't know how long. It felt like a pile of rubble fit to inter a corpse into, not a living soul.

I made him tea while he sat on the couch looking at the overcast skies. We smoked from sunset to sunup. By then we were just comfortable enough to approach what we'd seen.

"All this shit reminds me of Jack. He wasn't afraid of death. It still came for him," said Jeremy, as a plume of smoke ripped the silence apart. "When did we give up on life?"

"I haven't," I said. Jeremy passed me the bowl and coughed.

"I haven't either," he said, his voice choked with ash. "I know you feel like you're being strangled. You've got baggage and regrets weighing you down. I'll help you. Bring light and love to chaos and make it whole again, so that what caves in beneath you will sustain your step." I got up and dug into a small hill of confusion that had become obscure in the daze of recent years. Jeremy looked on amused for a while and then began to help. We worked and smoked through the night, replacing stillness and regret with sense and purpose.

"I'll always remember it wasn't just me getting my act together."

We left our tar-stained setup and sauntered into the bedroom as the canal people nursed their morning drinks. Jeremy burrowed into the sheets. He was soon invisible beneath folds of cotton, hiding from the dawn. He began to snore. I sat on the edge of the bed and watched the seagulls put on their morning act. I breathed in. I was alive.

***

I was staring at myself in the mirror. The receding liquor left me wide open for the horrors. I was staring at my own eyes in a mirror when he tiptoed behind me. His cold hands gave me a jolt. He took his hands off my shoulders and filled mine with a glass of pink lemonade and gin.

"A little gift from the dog that bit you. He's sorry." He trotted up to the drawn blinds with a drink of his own and stood there like David.

"Tell him he'll be hearing from my lawyer."

"The view's perfect... I have no idea what my neighbors are doing!"

"It's never occurred to you that you don't have to look out there?"

"And nobody knows what I'm doing either..." he whispered, taking a microscopic sip. I downed his potion and waited for relief to flow from my temples. I wrapped my arms around his waist.

"You wanna get out of here? Grab some drinks by the pier maybe?"

"It's ten thirty in the morning." He set a fifth of Sanguine Filth on the counter. "The pier doesn't open until eleven." He sat down on the couch and took a drink. I sat next to him and scrolled. I stopped at an article. John, presumed dead, was smiling at me from the thumbnail. I tapped his pudgy face and it expanded over the screen.

"Well yeah, Edith thought that was it for me, you know. I feel bad for making her cry. But praise God I'm alive!" I showed Jeremy. His face lit up with John's smile.

"No shit? He's alive! Fuck me, he's alive! Here's to John!" he shouted as he took another swig.

***

Terry and I were once in love with the same person. We could have made enemies out of each other and Eve miserable for as long as we were classmates, but we knew better. There was that unfortunate incident our first year of high school where I showed up at her place with a corsage and a hardcover edition of her favorite book and asked her to go to the winter dance with me. She had just said yes when Terry pulled up behind me. He still showed up, though sullen and dejected. He sulked in the back with the paper cups and ice water, but otherwise acted normally.

One morning after the semester was out, I got a phone call from Jeremy, who pulled a chest muscle from laughing too hard. There were pictures of me at the dance all over social media. I couldn't tell whether Terry was the worst photographer of all time or the best. His lens intercepted my face at exactly the right angles to make me look fugly as hell. What made the deal worse was my deliriously exultant smile. What other face could I have been wearing, dancing with the girl I liked? Anything else, were I not ignorant to the fact that I looked like a rat in glasses. I'm sure if he were to pull the same trick on me now it would bury any lingering suspicion out there that I was healthy, happy, making good decisions and living my life to the fullest. I untagged myself from all his posts and got dressed up to go to the movies with Eve.

So many things I felt in that theater have become impossibly strange. In my dress and grooming, I was the spitting image of a number of other young men in the room. I could actually sit next to her in those days and not feel like the floor was dropping out from under me.

"That was *terrible*," she said to the sunset.

"Yeah," I said after her. Translating my feelings into words seemed an unforgivable imposition. I cracked jokes until I got a ride home from my mom.

A few weeks later I found out Terry had taken Eve to a few concerts. They were small shows, in coffeeshops, with one guy and a guitar surrounded by flawlessly disheveled young people. The way he crooned into the mic, the way everyone swooned around him, the way they all shook with laughter to hear him sing about falling in love with a cellphone, it was perfect in her eyes. I had no idea she was as into music as she was. They showed up to the school talent show together in this cutesy little band they threw together. The way Eve looked on stage, like she'd died and gone to heaven.

I thought it was Terry who'd made her so happy, but really it was the chance to play music. She realized that she could be like that sardonic angel with the bowtie, vest, and mop for hair. Somehow, I made the determination to become something like that guy, someone who had wits, someone who may not have been clean-cut and pretty but wry, witty, and authentic most of all. When the time came to become myself that whole archetype had faded somewhat. I wasn't an artist, I was a tripster with a drinking problem. The prospect of failing her family and falling into poverty without their support had dissuaded her from exclusively pursuing any kind of artistic career.

Whatever connection I'd found with her, their connection was so much more real. I was determined not to be a dick about it. Then he became aloof, opaque, and intangible very suddenly in his seventeenth year. As his heart softened, he found friction everywhere. When word got out what exactly had happened with Terry, Eve's parents advised her not to see him.

Angry that he couldn't visit her at home, he got more possessive. She'd go to a show on her own or with a friend. He'd show up uninvited. Of course, he was fine to buy a ticket. They'd bonded over their musical interests after all. But the more aggressively he third wheeled the more like an outcast he felt. The tension between them built until, one night on a camping trip, she slipped into my sleeping bag instead of his. Terry was determined not to be a dick about it. By the time our senior year began he was asleep in a van in Oklahoma.

Of course, that was right around the time she got into tripping herself. There was I, desperate for her to notice me, as far from aloof as it gets. We had hobbies in common and I was grateful to share whatever time and warmth I had with her. We shared some strange times together and had moving words for our friends. She wanted to explore the world and I wanted to sit at home and enjoy the sure thing. The better we came to know each other the more we realized we would always be strangers.

11

Daylight pooled in Wallace's eyes from the petal lenses atop the SFO International Terminal. The folk ocean jostled him awake from the blue deep. He hid his wonder in his phone and found a lift. He refused help with his bags and slid into the back. He scrolled through his feed while the driver weaved through traffic. When he got out at his AirBnB, there was no goodbye. He looked at the wonderful old place, hands on hips, and wondered whether it was driving up the rent in his area.

"Better find an apartment soon. People will think I'm a tourist," he mumbled as he stacked shit in the bathroom. He headed down the street to a dispensary. He passed needles, prepared meals stacked by garbage cans, those afflicted with poverty, and armies of smartly dressed technomancers enjoying their gilded age. The bouquet of the sewers wafted over the fragrances of the impossibly rich, all sealed together with little tinges of dope and booze and flowers. Itinerant nutritionists ushered pamphlets into the hands of strangers while global fish stocks tanked. Anarchist bookstores waited patiently by burgeoning bars and cafés, where the public sat alone together. The dispensary was all marble and mirrors. Future funk echoed in the rafters. The sunlight's glare stood on his eyes in line. He left giggling at the variety of his catch: varietals old and new, strange and mediocre alike.

He hauled his goodies into the lair and staggered out for some pasta and wine. After pleasantries with the waiter he fished a few gummies out of a tin of Altoids and inhaled one. He choked and spat it across the room. He sank deep into his chair and disguised himself with the wine list. A livid gentleman stumbled by with half a spit soiled sherry sloshing a wayward trail behind him. Wallace staggered to his feet, offered apologies, and ordered a cocktail with some wine. His pasta dish came crowned with a delicious sauce with a base of squid ink, which he drowned in pinot noir. Little cutlets of the mollusc's flesh bobbed like lambs in a sea of blood.

He downed the rest of his glass and ordered another. Only the waiter, Gerald, wore a mask of tolerance. Marrow mousse hung off his whiskers as he asked about the reported novelty cocktails at hand. He tried to pay for the drink separately from the meal. Gerald explained that all of that would be handled with the bill. Wallace asked if he could have another drink anyway. Gerald skipped a beat and nodded. Wallace asked for a triple whiskey on the rocks. He picked at the packaging on another tin and pulled on a dab pen which he daydreamed was made of human bone. Not wanting to cause a scene, the waitress waited for him to leave so she could avoid a one-way conversation. He threw up the moment he stumbled out of the restaurant.

"Kneeling, hair sopping in the gutter, the great vomiter dies in the throes of creation," he thought. He hoisted himself back to life and dripped into a waiting ride. On his arrival home he was slumped over, having barely registered the trip. At the driver's urging he managed to roll out of the car and onto the sidewalk. Rain collected in his open mouth. For a moment there was silence, peace.

***

He moved into a lovely little place near Haight Ashbury, which he proceeded to destroy. His soon bottomless taste for expensive whiskey littered the hardwood floors with empty fifths and pints, mingled with the detritus of months of inactivity. There was a virtual library of frivolous receipts reposed on every available surface. He didn't want to know about the mold. All the sinks were clogged after three months. Whenever he went to use one, whether to fill up a bong or occasionally to wash his hands, he would first stick an unfolded paperclip into the drain to keep the sitting water level below the rim of the sink. There was always at least an inch of water in the basin. This and the blockage formed the perfect environment for fungal colonies to prosper in deep, dark blooms along the basin of the sink. The floors were choked with all the clothes he'd accumulated and refused to throw away over the years, the vast majority of which no longer fit. They almost carpeted the hardwood floors, tamped down by drunken stumbling and long hours on his back with a cellphone watching the room spin.

Every morning he lost the day before. His first three months in the city might well have been someone else's life for how much he recalled them. Though full of adventure, each one vanished like a vessel in the deep. He would call his mother whenever he was too sick to drink. He gushed about the city and filled the calls with reassuring, quotidian anecdotes. He took no notice of whether he was lying or telling the truth. His actual plans never filtered out from the static. He had no plans, no projects.

"I got some coding done," he said as he considered the stains on a beer bong.

"Well that's good!" she chimed. "I'll call you next week if I don't hear from you." When he didn't drink, his days invariably ended in a green coma. They were better than the great and terrible occasions wherein he would force feed himself a pint of grain ethanol and suck on carts until he forgot what he was doing. Food was expensive, rent was expensive, weed was expensive, booze was expensive, everything was expensive in San Francisco. His habits didn't break the bank. They broke him physically. The booze in particular did a number on his skin, his set, and his ability to jog uphill. It got harder and harder to know people when all his time slipped between his fingers. His vision trailed too much to look anyone in the eye. When he tried to be clever his wits dribbled down his chin.

Determined to see how far he could go, he went everywhere blasted; everything blasted back. Every morning he would wake up terrified that his life would always be a marriage of drugs and despair. Then he would spring out of bed to correct his own will against the change he knew he needed. He would charge through the bay in a blind fury of consumption past shadows he could not know. In the course of life, he was dead. In the course of the day he was asleep. His pain was only a memory. The moment was only a memory, and only for so long as it lasted.

He rested before a great concrete flower cathedral. The sound of trees almost blocked out the noise of cars. It was a white-knuckled afternoon of abstention. The bay-soaked half in sunshine and half in clouds. They rolled over mountainsides and wandered over the waters. The sounds of the city coagulated into one great hum. He relaxed into the grass and let his thoughts bloom. In the hum he felt a flower unfold somewhere between the end and the beginning of time. He opened his eyes and wept at the beauty of the world. He looked to his left. A man dressed in baggy clothes, well-worn and unwashed, sat slouching in the lotus position. He was, with impressive discretion, shooting up whatever adulterated powder he'd scored. Some dared to call it heroin, longtime users disagreed. Whatever he took into his veins, the man drifted into a peaceful nod. His gray goatee drooped with relief.

"Got any for me?" asked Wallace. The man didn't even raise his head to look at his cheeky smile. He just mumbled no.

While America toiled and spat in the heat of the grind, he sat aloft on clouds of vapor. He could afford to live in a city where too many were forced to commute. While his former classmates ran around solving problems, he sat around forgetting them. From time to time he would sit by the window and dream he was one of the techies or businesspeople who seemed to be too productive to transform their own abode into a remarkable shithole. Sometimes caught in a crippling hangover, he would stare through neighboring windows at young urban professionals fixing their business casual façades in the mirror and wish he had some deadline to meet or a boss to fear. He was a man without a master, save his own ungovernable appetites. They had him whole.

***

He passed a cloud of protestors with signs shouting, 'two jobs are enough' on his way to the dispensary. There was a man, likely their employer, staring down from the fourth-floor window with crossed arms and beads of sweat pouring down his face. Finally arriving, he presented his ID and declared that he was a regular. The bouncer nodded, apathetic. He went up to the counter and ordered a bunch of shit. Sitting down in a booth, he popped a pre-roll into his mouth along with some gummies. He lit the joint as he swallowed. After an hour he was only a little gone. He went back up to the counter and asked for a sheet of honey and a rig. After getting properly wired he left to finish out the day with a drink. He loved to frequent a joint in Little Italy by an iconic bookstore where he tended to drink himself into his customary midafternoon stupor.

He returned to himself on the bathroom floor. He didn't remember at first how he'd gotten there. The first lines of 'America' gently thrummed through the rafters. He remembered descending a staircase and got to his feet. Thank the heavens, he'd only slipped away for a moment. He hauled himself back up the stairs and clonked himself down on his stool and ordered an Irish coffee. He could hardly stay awake for more than five hours of a serious binge.

"I don't know whether I should just get a cab back to my room and wait this all out or not." The construction worker next to him thought a moment, and asked,

"How much did you take?" Wallace fixed him with an empty stare.

"Everything." He got a ride home after another drink and monologued incoherently to the driver. His face slid down the passenger's side window. "*Amazing, how did people know to put all this shit up?"* he thought to himself.

* * *

The next day he was apprehended in the course of his daily sleepwalk.

"Hey, are you looking for knowledge?" asked a tall shaggy man.

"I got comfort. I'm good," said Wallace. He walked on by. A hand came to his shoulder and jerked him back.

"Now listen, your flesh is only going to comfort you for so long. How about a joy that never ends?"

"All joy comes to an end, friend." He turned to look down at the massive digits curling around his shoulder blade and said, "But I'll see what you've got. What's your name?"

"Supposedly, I'm Herb."

"What?"

"It's short for Herbert. I swear it's not a nickname."

"No, I mean... What?"

"Right... It's written that when we talk about ourselves, we should say: 'supposedly.' It helps encode our views on individuation in speech and also works as a conversation starter." Wallace turned stoned as the daylights this way and that and asked,

"Conversation starter? How do you mean?"

***

They arrived at an old gothic building. Had it been a church at some point? It was jarring when he walked past a snarling gargoyle to find what looked like the perfume department in a dying shopping mall. An excellent man in a suit swooped in.

"Herb, this the new guy you were talking about?"

"Yep," he said.

"New guy?" asked Wallace.

"You're just in time. We're having another showing. Go and sit down in the theater, son." Herb rested his hand on the small of his quarry's back and led him into the darkened room. There they sat as an attendant brought them stale popcorn. The curtains opened and light streamed forth. The camera descended on a man approaching from the flapping curtains of a cardboard building.

"I'm the commissioner of the SFO branch. I'm pleased to welcome you all to the opportunity of a lifetime. Now, this may not be surprising to hear but the Academy is your friend. I can assure you, the wisdom we offer is the completion you seek. You could try to make it on your own, but this world will tear you apart eventually. You don't have to stumble around in darkness all your days. We don't want that to happen to you. We can save you from confusion. Not only that, we can take your confusion and make it into truth. The truth may be everywhere but HERE it's visible, in our books, at last. You are now among friends." Wallace glared into the sunset.

"That was stressful," said Herb approaching from behind.

"I hope you're not here to bother me more."

"Yes and no. I came here to give you a book, just in case you never come back here. I also wanted to invite you to dinner at my place."

"You cook?"

"Yeah, I got a nice place and that's how I enjoy my off hours. I don't mean to assume, but you don't seem like you get many home-cooked meals. Do you?"

"No, I don't." In his heart Wallace conceded to give the guy a shot. What had his palette not tasted? They walked uphill until they found Herb's building.

***

After showing off all his dab rigs, Herb sat him down on a space chair. Wallace began to thumb through the primer.

Axioms of the Academy:

The Notion of Unity: Inside and Outside, Self and Other are two aspects of the same thing.

The Notion of Mutability: All things constitute all other things. The nature of this arrangement precludes the existence of individual things, reality is instead an infinitely fine web of dynamic interrelationships.

The Notion of the Unspeakable: All truth transcends the bounds of language. Not even the Notions can accurately capture reality. All knowledge, all language occurs within the purview of truth as illusions, truth is the unsensible root of being in which all perceptions play themselves out.

"There are a ton of different teachers going around saying basically the same thing. Why y'all?"

"Listen, *I* know there's much more and much less to it than that. You know it too. I'm sure lots of people know it. But still, the paying public shows up and buys this crap like they need it. If they want to buy a taxidermy goat and call it a house pet, they deserve to be defrauded until they get wise. We make it look fun and easy like it's a game you can win. If truth can't even be defined it sure as hell isn't a game. That's the thing though: we all need something to get lost in desperately, something worth the candle."

"So, you mean, if somebody doesn't notice that these rules invalidate themselves…"

"They keep giving us money. The idea is they'll outgrow it eventually, some of them. Then they stay in to keep running the game on others. 'The fool who persists in his folly' and all that."

"You read Alan Watts?"

"Yeah, I read plenty of material outside the sanctioned Academy library. Honestly, the best material, the stuff they like to plagiarize the most, is exactly what they tell you not to read."

"So, okay, when do you start engaging the student honestly?"

"Well there's the thing, the Academy's all choked up with true believers. They believe, sincerely, that they have the best expression for inexpressible truth. We're here to offer people a way out of words by embracing just how far short of the mark they fall. It takes a while to figure out that if it's outside of the language game there are no failing marks, no sessions in the penalty box for a lifetime of confusion. *Everyone* is aware the pursuit of truth is horseshit, what they wake up to is how much time they've wasted talking about why. That *obsessive* apophatic treadmill is where we catch people, and bring them into our relentless qualifications of the word 'unspeakable.' In the corporate context it's all about maintaining a standard view that *everyone* can get behind. We can't be running after every parishioner's nuances. They bring their new ideas to us and we show them the way back to the standard view. We condition them to see the truth as ineffable, sure, but then we turn around and give them ten clever ways to tell their friends about it. We advance a script in the place of truth because we can no more possess it than those we mesmerize with our own empty words."

"That's tragic."

"If you're gonna get pissed with anyone, get pissed with me. Look, it's not immoral or anything. We don't own the experiences of our clients, and for the most part we don't create them. But the client can be influenced to believe so, and they are given an environment to question their inculturated thinking with others who are operating on the same new assumptions that they are. Too many people who peer into the abyss sink like stones. We'll be there to catch them."

"And any change that falls out of their wallets, no doubt."

"We'll be scrambling for that like nobody's business. Just being honest."

"So, since you take the notions at their word and toss them aside, what do you do to give yourself the jolt the written word was supposed to?"

"I've got a stack I've been working on. I always slip them in my food and get real fucked, start laughing and figure shit out."

"So, you're just a druggie like me?"

"In so many words…" Before the hour was out, he was howling at Herb's stories. "…And so, then he just rips into this Psych 101 textbook trying to explain 'operant conditioning.' He sat down to write an addendum before he forgot. He said it would solve humanity and bring peace to the world. He was so jammed at that point that he couldn't keep his train of thought straight, and he just ended up scribbling bullet points," said Herb.

"What did they say?"

"I don't remember. You have to understand, that was five years ago and I never saw the guy again, so..." They sat in silence.

"I haven't been honest with you, Herb."

"What do you mean?"

"Well, I knew about your whole Academy racket from the beginning. All your sitting me down and explaining this shit to me — well, it was cute is all I can say. My older brother, god rest his soul, knew a guy whose uncle is Emmanuel Hutch."

"The cornerstone?"

"That's right. I read the books your primers plagiarized. They were the only ones worth plagiarizing. I've read Hutch's recent crap. I've even read some of his unpublished manuscripts. Man's coming apart at the seams."

"No shit..." mumbled Herb, stroking his little beard. He leaned over the coffee table to take a hit off a stray rig.

"I think you owe me a little something for that information. I'm sure you'll get a kickback kicking that little tidbit upstairs."

"Sure, sure, take it and go ahead," Herb wheezed. Wallace drank in the vaporized honey shard and continued, "So... You know, you weren't the only one pretending."

"That was clear all along. You know, you might do well in a leadership position."

"Oh yeah? You'd hoist me up to your girder?"

"You'd share my spot in the sun." Wallace nodded at this.

"So, I'd have to pretend I care about a group I don't need, like you? All my life?"

"It's not that I care. I don't care. But it makes sense to me. I can sell it like I'm sold on it. If I can catch a thermal off this racket and fund my real dream, then so be it."

"What's your real dream?"

"A cabin in the woods, with all the latest conveniences of modern life, and a suitcase full of drugs to help me forget who I am."

"I would say that's giving up on life, but then I'd be hypocrite. It's the life I chose."

"Oh, you've got a cabin too?"

"N-no, no just an apartment," said Wallace.

"Oh," said Herb, who scanned him head to toe.

"I live the dream. In the summers I do. There's a little hamlet that all high-ranking Academy people and their kids visit. That's the life I want 24/7. Again, my dad's the commissioner. I'll never get kicked off the roles. I'll always have that cabin."

"Can I come and see it sometime?" asked Wallace. Herb smiled.

"If you promise to read this book and write me something explaining it back to me."

"Why?"

"It's part of your initiation." Herb showed Wallace the door.

"So soon?"

"I believe I've love bombed you enough. See you at the next meeting."

***

Months passed. Wallace awoke in agony. His phone was ringing. He squinted at the date, November 10, 2018. He suppressed a snarl as he answered:

"What?"

"...Hey buddy!"

"*Herb*? Haven't seen you in a while. Savannah? Congrats! What're you gonna be studying?" Just as they got going, a knock came at the door. Wallace hurriedly promised to call his friend back and stormed up to the door. He was still dressed from yesterday's romp. He swung the door open and there was Terry, looking happy and desperate at the same time.

"I left my car a few blocks down the street in some impossible place, prolly been towed... Hi, how are you?"

"You look about as tragic as I feel," said Wallace, turning back into his home for Terry to follow.

"I remember you sending me snaps of this place when you just moved in. I guess the usual happened?" asked Terry gingerly stepping over a tower of takeout boxes.

"The years got away from me," he replied, sliding a bunch of bottles off a ripped and stained armchair onto the detritus covering the floor so his old friend could rest his shaking legs. Wallace refrained to add that it was his drinking, not so much the years, that had gotten away from him. His night had become day, and his day had turned to night, to the point that to Wallace there was no longer any meaningful distinction. "What happened to *you?*"

"Oh..." started Terry, "...Same. Same. I was uh... I was living out in Bakersfield for a while, y'know, I had a band and all, left college to play out there and... Well, I guess I kinda fucked things up, or at least that's how they ended up." Terry sat up on the couch and kneaded his brow between his index finger and thumb. "Listen..." he began, "...I'm fucked out here. I've called up someone I still know from out east and she's offered me her couch, but I don't have any money to get out there..." Terry scratched the back of his head and held out his car keys. "The car's yours. It's beaten up, fucked up, and it's probably in a lot somewhere. If you can find it, it's yours. I just need money for a ticket back east."

"You're going back to North Carolina?"

"Well, I'll be staying in Asheville."

"What about home?"

"Nah... Nah, y'know, Hutch is there." Wallace dipped his head in recognition.

"That's more than fair."

"Have you heard anything from Jed? Jeremiah?"

"*You* were in that whole group. I was just Jack's little brother, y'know? I only ever knew what he told me. Now that he's gone... No, I don't know anything."

"That's fair." There was a long silence.

"I'll help you out man," said Wallace. "And have a smoke," he said, offering Terry dabs in a gesture of hospitality.

"Thank you. *Thank you,* said Terry.

"They might both be bad for my lungs, but I prefer the smoke in here to the smoke out there," said Wallace, taking a hit before passing the rig to Terry.

"Those poor people..." he exhaled before taking a hit. After coughing his lungs out, he wheezed, "It's been getting pretty hard to breathe out here."

"The smell of that smoke... It just fucking scares me man," said Wallace, cupping his head in his hands. "What can we do when we're so alone? I just look at that bridge and my guts fall out," he said. Terry remembered looking out a taxi window and seeing the Golden Gate bridge peeking out of the haze, menaced with a bloom of ochre sunshine. Behind it the fog stood like a monolith. The sun, the sea, and civilization glared through the murk searching for each other.

12

The sparkling rosé almost tasted sweeter coming up than going down. Almost. Since dawn I twisted in bed convinced I was dying of the flu or something. The hangover would end up being more vicious than I first expected. My last memory before falling asleep was downing the last third of a bottle and slumping into nothingness. My mind reeled at having to participate in my body's ordeal. Stillness seemed to provoke despair. Movement provoked the headache. I purged and crawled back to bed as the sun worked its way up into the late morning.

The first heave came like a friendly family pet ripping a gash in a guest. What did I not offer the shiny porcelain calf in my bathroom? I curled into a ball. Then I realized I had waffles with Eve at eleven. Tea, NSAIDs, and a brief bath helped, however, nothing would ever scrub out the memory of being strangled from within by acetaldehyde, the devilish fruit of the booze. I held my head in my hands and lazily poked holes in my egg until the plate ran over yellow.

"So, you're still getting drunk every night?"

"Yes," I said.

"You don't have any plans to change that?"

"No."

"Why?" she asked. I shrugged.

"I'm having fun. I'm young."

"You're 23 now, right?"

"Going on 24."

"And… Well, good for you." She rearranged the napkin in her lap and tapped her feet. "Do you remember prom?"

"We were such losers then…"

"I wasn't going to say it..." she said with a wry smile. She continued, "Even then I knew you could do better. Anyone could do better than that."

"What, eating too much to dance, drinking too much to talk?"

"Don't you like dancing and talking?"

"It was a priceless experience and a mistake. What else can I say?" I said.

"Yeah, but do you remember your head in the morning? Do you remember what a wreck your place was? You never invited that many people over again."

"Frankly, the decision was to make the night weird, damn the consequences. I've had thousands of nights I can't remember, each just like the last. The bullshit made it worth remembering. Do you always eat waffles with your exes?" I asked.

"What, I can't talk to a friend one on one?" she said, ripping her waffle in half with a fork and a spoon.

"Terry doesn't get weird about it?"

"You know I dump clingy men. People like that would be happier fucking a rusty pipe, at least that's something they could own," she said as she chewed off a piece of bacon.

"So, what do you want to talk about?" Her hand hovered over her plate, sending molasses streaming over the edges.

"Is Terry okay?"

"I mean..."

"Yeah, yeah, 'nobody's really okay,' I know that. It's just his reaction whenever he's on something serious scares me and he's *always* on something. It's so much worse than it was. He doesn't work and he doesn't help me with the apartment... I'm rethinking why I'm with him."

"So, love's not enough?"

"No... Look, I love *facets* of Terry. It's just that I hate living with whatever he's living with. It's getting to the point I dread seeing his face."

"That's kinda how I felt about you by the end." Eve seemed a little taken aback. If I'd said that a few years before she would've given me the cold shoulder for a week, whether it was true or not.

"Me too," she said. "Terry and I had a talk. I told him I was fine with him tripping so long as he wasn't flying off the handle. I'm used to this bullshit now, which is why if he ever touches that sap shit again, I'm dropping him."

"So…"

"If he trips again, and he does it with you, will you make sure he doesn't fly off the handle?" I nodded yes. "And I'm sorry about how we ended up strangers. I know you were keeping up some walls too. But I've got to acknowledge my part in the silence. I want us to move past it."

"I mean, haven't we?"

"It's hard to tell with you sometimes," she said and sipped. I scrunched up my eyebrows.

"What do you mean?"

"It can be really hard to tell if you mean what you say. It's scary never knowing what you're really thinking."

"Shit. I thought you could read me like a book."

"So did I." I took a bite of toast. "I could always tell you had boundary issues. You were so scared of turning someone away from you that you never considered whether you needed space."

"You know the reason we weren't talking?"

"What?" she asked, sipping iced tea.

"When people separate and cross over the horizon, they fuckin…" I scratched my forehead.

"They what?" She asked, chewing.

"They save face, you know? If they can't come across as

happy and successful, they try not to come across at all."

"And neither of us were happy."

"Right. Your life looked swank as fuck on Insta," I said.

"I made bank, then I got cocky and decided moving back here was a good idea."

"Oof," I munched.

***

"It's going to miss us!" Terry shouted. We all relaxed.

"Oh, thank God."

"We couldn't've taken another one like last year."

"Oh, we would've been fine. Evacuating would've sucked."

"Guess we're tripping after all!"

"Woah, what?" I leaned up.

"Shit, we forgot to tell him."

"We *forgot* to *tell* him! Jed, you want in?"

"What do I want?" But I already knew. I sat there for a moment pinching my chin. I looked at the dark sky with an eye of favor, of gratitude. I saw us all sitting comfortably in that abyss. Haltingly I said, "Just a little." I was handed a tab. I marveled that such a tiny piece of paper could consume me whole.

"Terry, d'you think Eve would want to join in?"

"She's sitting this one out. She said maybe later this summer she might jump back in. Is Gabriela coming?"

"She's building a treehouse."

"You're serious?" asked Terry. I swallowed my damp square. If I could just skirt by, I resolved to swear to never drop acid again like I had so many times before.

"Are they looking in here?" asked Terry.

"Don't start this again," said Jeremy with a magazine draped over his eyes, hands folded over his lap. I joined Terry by the door and parted the blinds with fingers.

"They could be... I thought I caught one of them staring at me from the staircase, but he was just talking to someone on the lawn. There are five of them milling around out there... All it takes is one glance," I replied.

"One glance for what?" asked Jeremy, incredulous.

"To become a witness, to seize power, leverage... The algorithm..." I stopped. I wasn't making sense. Jeremy heated up a bowl of chicken soup. The sheet draped over his shoulder looked like a toga. He sighed at Terry and I.

"They're Methodists on a field trip. They didn't go to the trouble of renting out that house just so they could watch you two tripping sack," he said.

"So what? They're still wired into the surveillance state, same as anyone... This house is surrounded... If we don't *move*..." said Terry.

"Let them be problems when they get problematic. Until then try to *get over yourself.* Know what I mean?" said Jeremy. He grabbed the last of the ginger tea from the fridge and took a big pull.

"Anxiety doesn't always respond to appeals for total acceptance. Sometimes it just won't budge," I said as I stared at three old men cracking up under the sun. Their energy was our own.

"Don't I know it?" said Jeremy. The voyager often contemplates the terror of being seized by the callous hand of an uncomprehending earthly authority in the course of shaking off conventional reality. This prompts them to consume, donate, or otherwise dispose of their entire stock so as not to incite the enculturated mindsets they so desperately wish to escape.

We decided that spending some time on the beach would do us some good. The instant we slid the door open, heat and color drew perspiration. The sun, in panoptic splendor, bore down on us with sustaining love, a free gift that kills like time. I was at once grateful and afraid. The idea of skin cancer nagged at me as we approached the beach access. I couldn't tell if it was laziness or fear that kept me out of the doctor's office.

We passed a tan van. A big guy in a trench coat stood by the driver's side door dicking around with a remote, big antenna wobbling in the Sea breeze. Terry stopped dead in his tracks to look at the man. An identically dressed companion emerged from behind the van with a remote of his own. Terry stepped back. A drone descended from on high a foot from Terry's face. His pupils shrank in fear as the drone's empty eye telescoped in on him. Jeremy grabbed him by the arm and tugged him along to the shore. Terry didn't even dare to look at the van people. He just stared ahead at the list of rules by the beach exit.

"I didn't like that," he said. Jeremy nodded.

"I bet you didn't," I responded to Terry's growing discomfort by rubbing his shoulder.

"You're gonna be okay man. Those were just some enthusiasts. They were just- recording… Us… And stuff."

"Do you think they're gonna follow us around with that thing?"

"Of course not," said Jeremy. So, we made it to the beach and headed straight to the pier. We removed our shoes and felt the wet sand work its way between our toes. I was doing biofeedback and tracing red-green ripples in spacetime. A gull would approach and stare bewildered. I saw peace and a sort of languid precision in those sun-glazed eyes. I knew I was among friends. I looked over at Terry.

He turned and gave me a wide smile as the wave broke

around his waist. Rivulets of water spattered my feet. He advanced into the sea, his fingers trailing after, as the sky crinkled like an aluminum afterthought. The Earth was dough beneath his feet, the water was a shimmering gem, and all around were his friends. He waded further, brushing past kelp and shells and, perhaps, a crab. He sank into the surf. The ages tore away and took flight. The dream was over. Light streamed into his lungs. He looked up to behold the faces of his friends. He felt our arms tugging him away from his sea bed. Jeremy slapped his back as our pal picked his way out of the lovely bright. Terry looked around at the throngs, waiting for their applause.

"How about some swimming?" he asked.

"Sure, but the peak is not the time," said Jeremy.

"Or the valley," said Terry.

We shepherded each other down the shore. I was reminded of a morning of mornings we shared by a cabin in the mountains. Terry stood proudly by the shore of a lake and announced that his fear of death was forever extinguished. The point he was trying to make couldn't be articulated in words. The tears pouring down his face said more. I remember the knowing nods we gave him, imagining that we had unexpectedly, finally attained something. We hoped to share our treasure forever.

To us the sweetest of truths was obvious, glaringly obvious. It was so obvious that the only way to mischaracterize it was to speak of it. This presents a problem for anyone trying to extract joy from the truth. What is freely offered can only be received without petition. We longed to learn from this silent perfection and drudged up many imitations of bliss in our efforts not to scare the truth away.

We learned that the medium through which all things exist was not, after all, a tool to be used or a goal to be attained. This truth gave us comfort. Life became a celebration. Our need for stillness had disturbed our stillness. To find stillness again we had to let it go.

We stepped gingerly over thick beds of seashells, feeling their little needles against our calloused soles. Because of our total focus, eyes cast down, we didn't see the dead shark until it was almost underfoot. Terry stepped back as we leaned in.

"Poor fella took a wrong turn somewhere," I said. Terry shivered at my remark. A fly zipped from the corpse to buzz at his ear. He swatted at it and took another step back.

"What did that to him?"

"What? Nobody. Nature did that," said Jeremy.

"I guess she'll do us all in?" asked Terry.

"Yes, I think that's her... purview," Jeremy replied. Terry shook his head saying,

"I don't want anyone else dragging me off this stage but mother nature herself. Just her," he said while stumbling back into an abandoned sand castle.

"I'm sure that's how it'll go down for you."

"Anything but being shrink-wrapped in a gene clinic... There's no chance of that, right?" Terry asked. He was crushing wads of wet sand between his trembling fingers.

"No, no chance," we reassured him. Terry smiled. I was relieved. For a moment, I saw my friend drawn away from Being by the shadow of death. We walked on. He started to ease up. The tendrils of water returning to the sea cut their riverbeds, echoing the flow of cirrus clouds. Above and below were reconciled.

Unfortunately, mother nature wasn't done fucking with Terry. We passed another dead spiny dogfish. Its tattered leathery skin opened into a broad dining hall for scavenging beachcombers. Terry looked into those corpse eyes and saw the unavoidable. The sight followed him as we passed.

"You don't think they poisoned the water, do you?" he asked

out of nowhere. Jeremy scoffed.

"Yeah, with generations of garbage and industrial byproducts," he said.

"So, it was a reckoning?" asked Terry.

"It was the shark's reckoning, comrade. Don't worry, you've been swallowing sea water since before you could talk," Jeremy replied. Terry nodded and began breathing deeply, holding it in, and exhaling slowly. I joined in encouraging him.

"Just remember, you know, you don't really exist in the first place."

"Right, right," he nodded. I felt like I was breaking decorum for bringing up selfhood.

"You were never born, you'll never die."

"Only a ripple in timeless dust," he said.

"Exactly."

"Like the shark."

"I mean... yeah," I said. Terry shivered.

When we found the third shark, a desiccated, rancid husk, Terry had had enough.

"This is a message or something. They've got complete control. They want to wipe us all out and start over again."

"Start what over again? The Bass Shack?" Jeremy gestured to the restaurant behind us.

"Those guys with the drones are up to something. Maybe they're dropping pellets of poison into the sea or maybe they're *collecting...*"

"What?"

"What if they want to haul us off to a deep sea black site and do fucked up shit to our eyes until we're old and grey and they squeeze us into the reef with the week's garbage?"

"I think we should get you home."

"Right, we'll be harder to trace there. I see your reasoning,"

Terry's teeth chattered. I sighed in relief when I saw that the drone brothers were no longer at their post outside the beach access. At this encouraging sign he nodded with approval and advanced confidently down the street ahead of Jeremy and I. I was astonished at his glow, after all his mind had done to itself. I assumed that our troubles for the day were over.

When home base came into view, we found a surprise. The Super Drone Brothers were parked outside my house. Terry sucked in air and grabbed my keys from out of my pocket. He sidestepped indoors, never taking his eyes off the two gentlemen at the helm. A drone zipped by and flashed a photo of him. His lower lip trembled. He walked on. As he closed the door he looked outside, only for the drone to catch another glimpse of his face. The door slammed shut. Jeremy waved at the still strange sight, imagining he was a niche micro-celebrity on a deep webcast.

Terry looked close to wigging as he scanned the horror show outside through the blinds. I gestured what the fuck at the dudes with the controls as they emotionlessly filmed every corner of the street in meticulous detail. They didn't notice me. The door of the neighbor's home slid open and out crept what looked to be a respected elder. He walked up to the boys without any salutation. One of them handed him a cellphone. He scrolled through, pausing to watch or read something a few times. He nodded and handed the phone back, and turned to give me a knowing look from across the street. Then he sashayed up the stairs. I never saw him again.

I'd almost forgotten I was tripping. Besides the grooves of chromatic convexity in my field of vision there were few reminders to be found. I was constantly imagining situations that would hilariously or horrifically spiral out of control, provoking the wrath of this or that neighbor, authority figure or deity. For the most part, I imagined Terry breaking first. The truth was, I was probably less stable than he was. He had the stubbornness to make it from Bakersfield to San Francisco, through Asheville to end up back in Sassoon on the kindness of friends. At Jedediah's door the flow of cosmic generosity stopped.

When Jeremy walked in the room it was like I'd never laid eyes on him before. He stole the whole show. We closed our eyes and hummed soundlessly with the gentle sloshing of the canal in the distance. I gave up looking for a revelation, for real this time, and let the trip slowly burn itself out.

"Okay, I'll talk," said Terry out of nowhere.

"What?" asked Jeremy, surreptitiously going for the shredded cheese in my fridge.

"How I lost all my money in Bakersfield." At this I leaned up out of my easy chair.

"Do tell," I said.

"Okay, so what happened was I met this swell guy at a bar. He tells me that he makes beats. And I was like beats? I wanna make some beats. So, we went back to my room and we got crossfaded and worked out a few prototypes before we hit on a sound. We developed our ideas, chose our samples carefully, and wove them into the narrative. We were doing well. I was surprised. Normally my drunk art is a mess. Eventually, he pulls out this absolute… shit he called 'sap.' We do a *tiny* little bit and before I blink, we have a whole album released on SoundCloud and the drapes on the hotel window are gone for some reason. We were getting some traction too, so we barreled on into day two getting ripped on all sorts of shit from his rucksack to stay awake basically and keep on making music. Eventually we crashed and I was out for a day. When I came to, he was gone. He left his laptop and his pants and left wearing mine. I think he was probably really sick and confused and ran off before he was cogent enough to realize he was wandering around the wilderness without any of his stuff. Poor guy. All I had was my car keys basically, and that little baggy of sap on his laptop. So, I drove to San Francisco with half a tank of gas and basically begged for whatever else I needed along the way. I texted Wallace for help, he was the only person I knew could help me west of the Sierra Nevada. He got me a plane ticket, the saint. We thought we were gonna shoot to the top overnight, no lie. Could been the drugs. When I found the album online, I realized we just made some spacey elevator music. Got a cult following though."

"It will probably outlive you." I looked at Jeremy, who added, "I didn't know that what happened to you."

"I'm not mad about it or anything."

"I thought someone just straight up robbed you blind. I'd be mad if someone did that to me," said Jeremy.

"They did, by accident."

"That's a helluva way to end a sojourn," I said.

"If I ever meet that man again, we're gonna make an album a day until we drop."

"What was it called?" asked Jeremy.

"Vandi Cliffs." Terry replied.

"You just made 'Vandi and Snype' one night? You?"

"With that guy, yeah."

"You invented a genre."

"Yeah... that was one helluva night." We all sat with that for a while.

"Did you ever find out what 'sap' actually is?"

"It's some pretty weird stuff. All I know about it is what I've felt, and personally, sap is the perfect name. I'm the sap. It's the con."

"Sure, that's one way to look at it. You think we should try to get a pharmacologist to study this stuff?" I asked.

"It's probably already in the literature. I think whoever's described it found sap's effects so debilitating that they assumed nobody would even think to use it recreationally. Nobody's ever found a medicinal application for this shit. So, it's not a controlled substance." Jeremy offered. "A fringe pharmakon, if you will."

"Literature? So, you mean the FDA might know what this shit is and have nothing to say about it being in the market?" asked Terry.

"Well, I didn't really mean *that* kind of literature. It probably really is unknown outside of the fuckass weird internet circles I run in," he replied as he texted.

"Maybe tryptamines don't give us what we want anymore because we're disrespecting them. We're not thinking about why we're taking them. Sometimes we're just charging in out of boredom. It's no wonder a lot of what we're getting is a weird... fucking mess," I said.

"How are we disrespecting them? We're putting a reasonable amount of thought into our doses."

"This often, with so little preparation... I'm not trying to be prescriptive. I just think we're not handling this stuff with respect. All this reckless bullshit smudges the lens we're trying to look through."

"Well Jed, the lens is supposed to be an illusion anyway. It getting smudged only tells you that the image coming through is an apparition. Besides, I thought you said fun was the perfect way to learn."

"For the record, I did *not* have fun today," said Terry, bursting out into laughter. I smiled. But when I went to bed, I still felt deep exhaustion, a pricked conscience, and smarting welts of old wounds unhealed by the day's events. I was still grasping after something, precluding peace. I was going in too often for my own good. I was being disrespectful. Whatever wavelength Jeremy was on, it was keeping him abreast of the fear.

***

It was one of those rare afternoons where it was just Gabriela and I shooting the shit on a swinging bench. Light sucking clouds of darkened rain began to consume the sky and pelt the earth with nourishing water. She held up her phone trying to record the sounds of seagulls. We walked inside when a blast of heavy wind prompted us to. We sat around wondering what to do.

"I wonder…" she said as she got up and pulled a drawer out.

"What?"

"Which of us can out smoke the other." She tossed me what looked to be an eighth and change of flower for my inspection.

"Well shit, I mean it depends right?"

"On what?"

"Where's your tolerance at?"

"I got this bag two days ago and it's halfway gone. I want to have a memorable experience with the rest."

"You could always wait a week or two before your tolerance goes back to normal."

This stuff has a reputation that precedes it. No fancy name, just a few nicknames, open sunlight, and living soil. I know you're into getting your thoughts well and truly stuck into loops. This will facilitate." I nodded, beginning to examine the buds more closely for any delightful inflections of eccentricity. "Shall we begin?"

"No time but the present, as Jeremy would say…"

Thunder rumbled in the distance. Clouds fired like steam exhaust from an old locomotive. The rain quenched the ground as my mouth became scorched and dry. Little flecks of red and green began boosting themselves out of the grays and blues of the darkened day. The proud succulents on her desk seemed to expound on the mysteries of the multiverse. Grains of sand arrayed on the concrete outside urged patience. Everything gestured with its whole being. What statement was I making, laughing hysterically on the floor while Gabriela sang playing an electric viola like a harp?

When we realized we'd run out we laughed harder than we had ever laughed before and went staggering out by the waterway, getting caked with mud and sloshed with rain. We called out to passing ships and they called out to us. Gabriela passed out at her desk, trying to come up with a playlist for the rest of the day. I went out drinking rain, splayed under heaven. We remembered the walk we took, but it was years before either of us recalled the viola.

13

Jeremy looked at his smart brick with a deepening frown.

What is it?" I asked. He showed me a rambling text from a Bay Area number promising some big shindig in the mountains.

"I think I know who sent this," he said. I nodded into empty air. Jeremy got another text from the same number. "It *was* Herb. He just sent me a time and an address... Huh..." Jeremy sat down.

"What's up?"

"Amarna. That's the Academy's hamlet for bigwigs. My dad had a place there once before I got kicked out."

"You never mentioned staying there."

"I never got to. I got the summer program. They've got this weird little camp up there. I broke the rules same as anyone and I'm the only one who got treated like shit."

"I didn't realize Herb was in so deep with the Academy. You feel okay about being in one of their spaces again?"

"Honestly Jedediah... I'm kinda down to mooch. How do you feel?"

"Herb was pretty fun. There's a lot we don't know about him." I said.

"We'll see about Herb, Jed. Rest assured. Think anyone else is gonna be down? I'd rather not be crowded out by Herb's faction if I can help it."

"His faction? You think it'll be like that?"

"He's probably high up in the in-group too. The Academy

tends to see outsiders for their usefulness. Sure, they're inviting at first, but once the mark is full of free cake, he starts coming on with demands... I've love-bombed people to recruit them before. It's alienating in the end. It's conditional love in the end, counterfeit. Before the lonely sap knows it, they're on that endless distribution treadmill."

"If he just wants to hang out, we can always say no to anything else."

"When you're recruiting, you're only nice when you still have a chance of winning someone's soul. He must have special privileges if he's cavorting like that in Savannah. I bet he's out there to 'meet people where they're at' or something."

"Do you think Gabriela would be down?"

"She'd be down for a weekend of hiking and chilling; unless she's started whittling 'Chibi Charles Darwin.' What about Terry?"

"Well... he's still trying to work things out with Eve, right?

"Yeah, exactly."

"The last thing that relationship needs is a vacation," I said.

"Maybe, but it could be exactly what they need as individuals." I tried to figure out his angle. "Hey, I *really* don't want to be outnumbered up there. I *really* don't," he said.

"It's not like they'll be drawing lots on who to eat. We'll be fine. And if you're that scared you don't have to go, Jeremiah."

"No, I'm down. Are you down?" asked Jeremy.

"Yeah. Of course," I answered.

"Okay, I'm down."

"We're inviting Eve and Terry though."

"Oh Lord."

***

We assembled before daybreak, inflating tires and the bags under our eyes. We packed ourselves in like sardines and coasted along the empty streets at dawn. Gabriela sat between Terry and Eve, enduring the bad blood circulating between the two. Their latest armistice had already crumbled into sand. Their voices were so hoarse that they hardly said a word.

"Y'all comfy back there?" asked Jeremy from behind the wheel. When he got no response, he turned up the dreampop and leaned over to whisper to me, *"I think they're mad."*

Gabriela asked if she could light up. Jeremy assented. Eve stared into the back of Jeremy's head, fists crumpled on her knees. Gabby burned the end of the cigarette and handed it to Jeremy. He tasted it and handed it back. His lipstick was miles darker than hers, leaving an impressive mark on the filter.

"I'm hungry," I said.

"Me too," said Terry.

"There should be a Meister Burger somewhere around here," said Eve.

"That place gave me some kinda awful disease, like a bowling ball in my gut," said Jeremy. We were silent. He relented and drove us to the Meister Burger. Their corporate mascot was really hard on the eyes. The facsimile Burger Meister was curled around the store logo smiling crooked like some cartoon Mephistopheles. There was a horrible gleam in those glazed, plastic eyes.

"I feed my customers to my customers," they seemed to say. We got our food. I put mine on the console and rested my eyes. "Is it normal to imagine a freight truck flying across the median into my windshield?" asked Jeremy. Nobody said a word. He continued, "It's been happening a lot lately. Chill hop or synthwave?" He looked at the grumpy travelers crunched up in the back. Soon I was asleep. When I came to, I saw Jeremy munching away at my burger sheepishly. "Sorry." I shrugged and tried to go back to sleep.

I heard my friends hollering when we caught sight of the mountains. The mountains are honored by their beauty. They are anointed with rain. They are endowed with age. They are brimming with life, and may they for an eon more. Docile behemoths towered over every gas station, eatery, traffic light, church, and PC repair store. Everywhere plants forced themselves up through boulders and pebbles. The earth mothered up trees and stones and rivers and people alike. The truth was always clear; if we go, the mountains stay.

***

We turned off the highway down a perilously steep trail to find a fenced-in collection of wooden cabins. Jeremy sighed when he saw the little sign out front spelling 'Amarna.' Beyond was a squat green mountain just beyond the bend. It bent toward him in a jaunty tilt and lilted wearily at him. He looked away, at passing valleys, at people, at grocery stores and billboards.

"Should we turn back?" he asked. Eve exhaled slowly and touched her forehead to the headrest in front of her. We got out and stretched our legs. The Edenic fragrance of mountain air abounded. We held our breath as we walked to the front entrance of a particularly nice cabin.

"This must be the place," said Terry. Jeremy called Herbert in vain. We circled the glossy little homestead. I peered through one window and saw Gabby peering through another. There was a shadow sitting in the corner. We knocked. The stranger opened the door. He lacked the eye bags of a run-of-the-mill Academy shill but wore a different sort of exhaustion in his posture.

"Wrong place," he said.

We apologized and backed off in a breeze of huffs and puffs. The man shut the door and parted the blinds to watch us leave.

"Where the hell is he?" Terry whispered. We shuffled around, reluctantly patrolling from house to house for the right sign. There were bronze statues of various founding members of the Academy. Hutch's absence was noticeable on the empty base in the middle of the hamlet's dirt crossroads. I imagined we were being watched. The river's rush chastised us for feeling uneasy in such a beautiful place. I remember writing the whole trip off before I even decided to go.

We had almost given up hope of finding our dazed acquaintance when we saw him sauntering over to a vending machine by a condemned indoctrination center. He pulled up his loose-fitting pants and snorted. He only noticed us when Terry put a hand on his shoulder. There was an instant of confusion drawn across his face before recognition dawned.

"You *actually* came?" he asked.

"...Yes... If there are too many of us, we can always get another room somewhere else," said Jeremy. Herbert scanned us all.

"Don't be ridiculous. All are welcome here." He began leading us up the stairs as he explained what he had for breakfast that morning.

"I got this stuff off the deep web, it's called 'Ichor?' I heard it's some really nasty shit but I've just been microdosing it and fwooooaaaaaaaahhh..." Herb brought a baggy of a familiar substance to eye level and began shaking it. Eve turned and started walking to the car. Terry followed quickly after.

"What the hell?" he asked.

"Don't take that tone with me," she said.

"What's wrong?" asked Herb.

"He's got sap. I can see where this is going. This is not the kind of trip I signed up for."

"Well he didn't say anything about *using* it!" shouted Terry. Eve turned to look at him. Then she turned to look at Herb.

"Can't you just wait until we're gone to break that stuff out?"

"I do what I want and I *share* what I want in my own place." Eve nodded slowly and turned to Terry.

"If you lose yourself again, I'm leaving. I am calling myself a ride and I will be out of your life before you can say 'groovy.' I came out here to relax and to smell the fresh air. I didn't come here to watch people eat poison and total cars," she said. She closed the door to Jeremy's car after pulling the rest of her stuff out of the backseat. Herb nodded, taking it all in. He was probably thinking back to his only other exposure to Eve: Terry sobbing into his phone down in Savannah.

"Okay, okay I won't take any while you're here," Terry breathed, even to his surprise. "See? I can do right by you," he said as Eve brushed past him and through the front door.

***

I took my last good look at the highway before entering Herbert's enclosure. It was a dank place, mist hanging from the ceiling. Out of the far window was a broad and grooving glenn. Before us a gloomy den of human comforts. We happened upon a room suffused with gray light, complete with a cornucopia of glassware, empty bowls, and a sleeping bear of a man splayed out on the couch.

"Holy shit, Wallace?" Jeremy stopped in his tracks.

"This is the first time he's slept in two days, I'd let him be," Herbert advised.

"Wait, Jack's brother Wallace?" asked Gabriela.

"Yeah, the one who went out west," replied Jeremy.

"Why's he in a cult?" asked Gabriela, poking Wallace.

"I wouldn't call it a cult, it's more of a... a load of really dedicated people," said Herb.

"Wordless truths don't need in-groups and out-groups," said Jeremy.

"Well, I hope we can show some of the positive sides of... being in community, sharing in the now..." Herb mumbled, visibly uncomfortable. Terry let loose a set of deathly retching coughs. The dab rig slipped out of his hands and shattered across the floor. He scrunched down to get it together, clouds billowing out of his nose. The blood had already drained from Herb's face. I was still cooling off from my recent psychedelic fuckbungles and decided I'd rather be silly drunk for the whole weekend than participate in any shenanigans. The fact that Herb partied with research chemicals wasn't too surprising given his past behavior. That he had such shitty taste was a revelation.

"I'm telling you man; the whole point is not to get distracted by the end. The means must be the end. You must learn to harmonize with your desired endpoint so that they become the same," said Herb.

"You can't just sit in the mud and teach yourself to love it," said Jeremy.

"Yeah but that's what got us into trouble, drawing distinctions, the knowledge of good and evil. The fruit fucked us up; we've got to throw it up," Herb insisted.

"We were meant to lose our place in the garden. To have any future at all the past must die. To live at all, death has to factor in somehow," said Jeremy.

"What the hell are you guys *talking* about?" asked Terry. Wallace stirred beside him. He sat up and fixed Jeremy with a look.

"Hey man. Long time no see," he said. Jeremy smirked.

"I see you made it out too. Didja get that job?"
"Got close. Life happened, you know how it is."

***

Herb, on a whim, decided to save the trip for the next day and take us out to a little tavern. He showed the best of his gregarious spirit, holding a mug aloft proclaiming this and that. Terry and Eve spoke some, but not much, as could be expected from the deep wedge between them. I surmised, over Scotch eggs, that it was Eve wanting to live one way and Terry another. We stumbled home and bade one another good night, retiring to separate beds in mostly separate rooms. For the rough and tumble vibes Herbert gave off, he was an unusually diligent host with an unusually large number of guest rooms.

Dead awake at four a.m., I wandered onto Herb's back porch. Gabriela was the only other person up. She had a nice work set-up on the glass coffee table to the left of the door. I saw sketches of the mountain vista before us and a grinder balancing a ball-point pen.

"Can't you sleep?"
"It's hard to sleep when I don't drink."
"Jed, you've been drunk all day."
"I feel like shit."
"Well, we've run out of liquor."
"Already?"
"Oh yeah," sighed Gabriela. I sat down across from her on the back porch and looked at the moonlight over the peaks and valleys forested in gleaming black. The low-hanging clouds reflecting the palest flame back at us completed the painting. It still hangs in my mind. "Why *did* you and Eve break up?" she asked.

"Jeremy knows more about those days than I do. It's hard to remember much from the breakdown. It's a blur. I'm sure Eve knows what pushed her away."

"What pushed you away from her?"

"I realized too late that I'd given her the switch that makes me happy or sad and I wanted to get it back without hurting her feelings… Or mine. I went my way as best I could but all the time I was compromising. I let those moments she made me feel whole justify sticking around. I guess exile at sea was preferable to separation. Jeremy calls it a 'codependent' something. I was still full of hollow affection. Could I tell her I couldn't wait to leave her bed in the morning? I lied and said 'I will always love you.' So, she left. Wouldn't you, if you handed over your heart for counterfeit love? I had a GPA to service and an ego to placate and friendships I'd die to still have. I was twenty-one, y'know? I wanted to do everything at once. From the second I woke up to the moment I fell asleep I was on a track. I was burning out and I didn't know it. I got spread so thin I was all surface and no substance. I just fucking dried up and blew away."

"You just used to pretend a lot more than you do now. You should talk about this shit more often though. I've been there, Jed. I cared way too much once. It's bad news. I put more effort into helping others than I ever did myself. Took me to a bad place."

"I'm sorry to hear that."

"So, you broke down a while back and it's taken time to piece yourself together, longer than you'd like. You're gonna spend the rest of your life putting yourself together. That's all any of us can do, even if you could be perfect there's no getting there overnight."

"What's keeping you down?" I asked. Gabriela thought for a moment.

"What I think my peers think of me. Not even what they actually think of me. I'm the best at hurting my own feelings, I guess. I judge myself for being an artist. Sometimes I have to sit and actively remind myself of all the positive shit I usually ignore." We said goodnight. I passed the room where Terry and Eve were sleeping and heard voices. They had hardly spoken on the first day of the trip. He would look at her and she would look away, she would look at him and he would pretend he was staring out a window.

"You're all I have, Eve," said Terry. I heard him pulling her close.

"It's always going to be weird… I never meant for it to be this way…"

"Neither did I." There was silence. I stifled my breathing and decided that eavesdropping was wrong. I felt awful for giving Terry the impression I hated his guts.

"What if I asked you to marry me?" he asked. I stopped.

"What kind of question is that?" she asked. I walked away as slowly as I could.

I went back to my single bed in the guest room and looked at Jeremy draped over a plot of sunshine in the pre-dawn gloom.

***

I dreamt I was an old man rocking my chair and sucking white whiskey out of a little kettle giddy for the coming oblivion. I sipped, smacked my lips, swirled the saucer and sauced myself again and broke out into a haunting giggle. I collapsed. Cardinals picked every speck of dust off my carcass.

When the wrath of last night's liquor hit, I woke up and threw up over the balcony onto the parking lot below. Jeremy laughed. I turned to see him with a cup of coffee. He handed it to me and we chatted about places we hadn't been.

14

We sat around as the afternoon ripened and began to turn. Wallace sat before me stuffing dank into a porcelain basilisk. It looked more like a French horn made of glass than anything you might smoke out of. If it weren't for the tar water stewing in the basin, I would have assumed it was an experimental art installation. He beckoned me over and I gingerly took the lighter from his waiting hand. I pulled for maybe five seconds before dissolving into a coughing fit that had me on the floor. When I got up, I had to sit down. What was this unearthly feeling? I felt well and truly stoned for the first time in a long time. Years of living on mids down in Brunschweig county had left me wide open for a frenzied ambush to play on my senses.

"What does it say about me that I spend most of my time watching someone play a video game instead of playing one myself?" asked Wallace. Herb's flatscreen was playing a stream of some guy sucking at Doom.

Herb laced his fingers together to contain his nerves. Unable to stand the silence, he said: "Let's go to the river."

"River?"

"Well we're not gonna blast off *here*. It's cramped. There are people all around us, not to mention all these fuckin' electronics and shit." Jeremy nodded reluctantly, looking around at the giant stuffed bear, the couches, and the enormous kitchen. He said:

"Look, I have really, *really* sweet blood, the mosquitoes are gonna kill me out there. I just thin."

"Stay here then. I don't care. I go my way. You go yours," Herb interrupted. His tone indicated a pit of derision smoldering deep inside of him. Or was it the hangover lacing all his words with venom? He grabbed a bag and poked Wallace out of a trance, saying: "Yo, we're heading to the creek. You wanna come with?"

"Absitively. Gimme a sec." He stretched, looking deceased and reborn all at once.

***

For a guy concerned about his carbon footprint, Herb drove a monster of a car, able to fit all seven of us inside. The ride wasn't so tense. We were no strangers to two lane roads winding around the side of a mountain. As we rounded a corner a long valley underscored a great range of blue and green. Its peaks danced to our right decked out in the most astonishing array of forest, stone, water, and human trapping I had ever seen. I simply wanted to live there for the rest of my life.

Herb drove, vaping the whole way. We were all a bit on edge. I was so drained that my mind couldn't penetrate beyond the bare surfaces of things to glean any meaning underneath. I caught snippets of dialogue as we trudged along to the treeline from a gravel parking lot. My muscles began protesting once we reached the level of the creek and went skipping our way over the rocks. I dipped my left hand in the cool current and closed my eyes. By the time we'd settled in the jagged shade of a stand of rocks in the stream, our ideas outnumbered the beats of our hearts.

"We always harp on about the consequences of being lorded over by our failures but aren't there consequences for defining ourselves by our successes? You might be comfortable right now but just know that the easy chair is not where true happiness is.

It's out here, where the river flows, where your comforts beg for you to return from far away and you justly, wisely stay away. Yes: with this taste of nature I have finally society-proofed myself," said Jeremy.

"Here's to the new decade... I'm already shivering."

"Time is fucked."

"Time isn't real. It's an old delusion. We've got to let it go. We gotta wake up from history if any of us are going to survive," said Herbert.

"You'll find it's quite persistent," said Jeremy.

"Prehistory was weird. You ever hear of gigantopithecus?"

"What?"

"Gigantopithecus man, largest primate there ever was. If we got the bigfoot archetype from anywhere in nature it'd have been from dorky nomads stumbling across them in a forest clearing. Imagine it," Jeremy passed to me.

"Sounds pretty... Pretty memorable," said Terry."

"Totally, these guys were like... HUGE man. Fucking gigantic," he replied.

"We're gonna go for a quick walk over that way," said Gabriela as she started to the far bank of the creek. Eve followed.

***

Something about the stillness of nature around us prompted Jeremy to go up to Wallace and get something off his chest.

"Man," started Jeremy, barely able to hold the tears back after a lull in the conversation. "Wallace, if I had known how... How dangerous 25i was, I wouldn't have taken it. I would have warned your brother not to take it," he said as he hung his head and began to shake."

"If I'd known... Me too... You know I don't blame you for

what happened, right?" Wallace asked, wiping his eyes.

"I know, I know," said Jeremy, but he wept silently nonetheless, able to forgive himself after so many years. In the summer of 2015, we'd received news that Jack, a classmate and friend, had died in his home with it in his system. 25i-NBOMe has unpredictable effects on those who take it, having been synthesized only recently and marketed on the gray market. Unlike many of the substances people take in its stead, 25i has a potential to kill at very low doses. It was a shock that ruptured the entire community. We vowed, Jeremy, Terrence and I, to practice caution around what we consumed. As with a fair few things, we failed to honor that oath. Any time our tabs were bitter though, we'd spit them out. We practiced that unquestioningly. We looked around to see that Gabriela and Eve were still gone on their walk.

Gabriela and Eve emerged from the trees into an open grove.

"Here?" she asked Eve.

"Yeah, yeah this spot looks okay." They both sat down. Gabriela started rummaging around in her rucksack. "Herb is something else, hey?"

"His heart's in the right place. I think. He's just… troubled."

"I'll say," said Eve, "he thinks the stars above are rings around his head. He thinks he's the goddamn chosen one."

"Maybe we're all chosen."

"By whomst? God?"

"I dunno what you mean by that word, but if there's choosing going on God's as good a word as any."

"I didn't know you believed in an intentional universe."

"Maybe not intentional, not in the linear way you and I seem to be. Intelligent though? Yeah, the universe is pretty fucking intelligent."

"I don't think he likes it when women have opinions."

"Herb?"

"Who else?"

"That's exactly why you shouldn't take his pontificating shit. He sure as hell isn't the first latent misogynist to get up on a big high trippy horse to preach to the masses and soothe his fragile ego. He's an open wound who'd rather be exalted for getting barbecued on a ten strip than face himself as he really is. Listen to this instead." Gabriela produced a small plastic baggie with a nugget of translucent orange goo.

"Is that…?"

"Dimethyltryptamine. They used to call it 'telepathine.'"

"Fuck… I didn't think it'd be orange."

"Do you want some?"

"Maybe just a little…"

"Try it with this." Gabriela pulled out a jar of what looked to be tea.

"You've been doing a lot of work on yourself. Growing. Reflecting. I think you'll be fine if you do a little exploring," said Gabriela.

"You want me to mix those two together…? I'm still stoned from this morning."

"I mean hey, if you're nervous you can just do a little. You have nothing to prove."

"Try telling that to Herb. Nobody's experience is valid if it isn't pushing some record."

"Herb can jump in a lake. Just because tripping's a big pissing contest to him doesn't mean a little dose can't teach you something." Eve eyed the little pipe Gabriela produced.

"Oh god, that's another thing, he'd say we needed a glass base pipe. He'd say we're wasting a precious molecule with our impure methods."

"All you're doing is giving his judgmental shit a platform in your own mind. Doesn't that give you a fucking headache? You're not a devil because you don't have a fucking freebase pipe. You're just making do," said Gabriela as she painstakingly put a little glob on a cashed bed of ash. "Here, I'm gonna take this hit. Sip this tea some. And remember: the key to a successful DMT trip is surrendering yourself to death."

Eve rubbed her temples.

"Are you okay?" asked Gabriela.

"I got this crushing fucking headache out of nowhere."

"Are you dehydrated?"

"Oh fuck, that must be it. I've been hauling this gallon jug the whole time."

***

A lull came over the afternoon. We piled back into the car after reuniting. We sat silently under the dusty light of mountain vistas as we returned to Herb's. As all seven of us piled back into the house, we waited for Herb to force the ichor issue. Eve threw her stuff in a bag but stopped at the entrance. She put her bag down and sat down next to Terry. Herb was determinedly focused on measuring out safe doses of sap, a powder finer than flower, with his bare hands.

"Let's all take some together," Herb suggested. Terry sat up and smiled.

"Don't put us through that again," said Eve. She went straight into bargaining with someone who was, in her eyes, fixing to bungee jump into a black hole.

"Don't make decisions for him, Eve," said Herbert.

"And you, *helping* him destroy himself and messing yourself up in the process. Why did you invite us all out here?"

"I can show your friends that if they join us, they will never be alone."

"That's not how that works," said Jeremy.

"The truth will always be with us. I know just how to show you all," said Herbert through gritted teeth.

"I don't think I'll join. How'd your trip go?" asked Terry. Eve tried to relax.

"Well, I sat still and looked at the pine needles…"

"That sounds fucking amazing, Eve, but You can't just stick your toe in the water and say you're a psychonaut. You have to *earn* that title," said Herb from his lounging spot on the couch.

"Well what does it matter what you think?"

"What does it matter? I do more DMT than anyone I know and I know how it should be done." Jeremy burst out laughing.

"Oh my God, Herb, could you be any more fucking egotistical?"

"What ego? I destroyed my ego. I took a ten strip on ketamine once. I've eaten more shrooms than you can collectively handle."

"Isn't the point of doing psychedelics to get over yourself?"

"It's to *achieve* higher and higher levels of consciousness and enlightenment."

"Yeah? And just who is it that acquires wisdom like a Mazerati?"

"At least he's not telling people what to do," said Terry sheepishly.

"What?" asked Eve. Terry grabbed a dose from the table and looked her in her blue eyes.

"I can do whatever I want."

"You're going to lose me. I can't stick around waiting for you to start valuing the things you can't replace," said Eve.

"If it means I get to do me, then I'm happy."

"But we… Well… I'm leaving then. We talked about this.

I'm *gone.* Terry, *fuck* you!" she said, trembling with fury, tears falling off her chin.

"A good partner would never say shit like that!" said Herb.

"I'm not his partner anymore. I just... I just want to go home..." said Eve, walking through the door and stamping her feet with every step to the road. For a second she stomped back to hurl: "Like *I* didn't give up an *arm* and a *fucking leg* for you, *Terry!"* Terry followed Eve out the door to the curb, hoping for one last chance to change her mind.

"Eve? What about what I promised?" asked Terry as she slammed the door. I sighed and walked into the kitchen as Herb talked on like nothing had happened. Jeremy poured schnapps into a little glass for himself. Eve waited for her ride. I walked outside to say goodbye.

I found her outside in the cold, phone in hand. She smiled and then opened her mouth, "I want to like you all... But sometimes we're all just too much. Maybe it was a mercy, us being total strangers to each other."

"Sometimes I don't like me either," I said.

"I don't want to be like you. Any of you. It's weird, I came back here to connect with my old life. I never thought *I* would be the one to jinx that. I changed, and I can see y'all haven't." Despite the content of her goodbye I couldn't feel any animosity coming from her. Standing alone out there in the reminded me of the shrill fall days we would walk by empty labs with gorgeous walls of glass.

"I think about you every day," I said, without realizing what I'd said.

"I did too. I understand now why you didn't see a future for us," she said. Her ride pulled up and she headed to the nearest car rental. I heard Terry sob in the kitchen. Herb laughed to himself as Jeremy and Gabriela drank and played cards.

***

The morning light was deceptively kind. Our host stood patiently by a few sizzling pans on the stove.

"Breakfast, friends, breakfast, but with a bigger picture in mind," he announced. Jeremy yawned and got to his feet.

"Scooch on over Herb, I'm gonna make an omelet," he said.

"No."

"What?"

"No, I'm using this stove for pasta."

"At… nine a.m.?"

"*Yes. Step off.*"

"There's room for two in this saloon Herb," said Jeremy. Herb looked around the room and then at Terry, who was still somber and silent. "Just let me…"

"*FUCK OFF!*" Herbert shouted as he threw the boiling pasta water on the ground. We were all burned, except Gabriela who sat thinking in the living room. We all got profuse apologies as we promptly packed to leave in short order.

"I'd like to share a little piece of advice before you go," said Herb. He had abandoned simple apologies as futile.

"I don't want to hear it," said Jeremy.

"No, it's good, I just wanna tell you something."

"I don't want to hear it."

"Stop waiting for other people to understand you. Otherwise you'll wait forever to be happy." Jeremiah thought for a moment.

"I'll forgive you for that lovely piece of unsolicited advice. Now, I am going home and having a long smoke with my friend. Good day Herbert. Thank you, Wallace."

"Peace brother," said Wallace.

"Come along, Jed, we're getting a *real* breakfast." I trotted out after Jeremy. Gabriela stood by the car sketching the nearest peak on the last few pages of her summer notebook. Herb stopped Terry at the door.

"Dude."

"No," said Terry.

"Dude, let me give you 1000 dollars."

"Absolutely no- what? Why?"

"I heard about your situation…"

"Fuck, how? Who? Man, okay, listen I'll be fine. My friends have my back. Eve's gonna be better without me."

"Aren't I your friend?"

"You're… You're my *friend*, sure, I just don't want your *money*."

"Let me help you. I promise I don't pity you."

"For what? I'm just *moving out,* it happens."

"I was once put in a vulnerable position like you. It was a breakup; I had to stay at a friend's for a while. He was nice to me, and I wanna be nice to you. Let me be nice, man." Tears began welling up in his eyes. He said, "I feel like shit right now. I have to be nice to someone."

"Okay… Okay I accept. How are we gonna…?"

"I'll just, uhh… Mail it to Jed?"

"Okay, thank you, thank you… Thank you Herb," said Terry, shaking his hand earnestly and looking him in the eye.

"It's nothing man. Thanks for hanging out, you know, and thanks for forgiving me and… and being able to look me in the eye and…"

"Yeah, yeah man."

Herb stared into the sunset watching us drive away into the forest. Wallace stumbled onto the porch and fell to his knees, waving goodbye with his last ounce of strength.

"Grab the blowtorch Wally; we're going in tonight," Herb

commanded as he marched back into his abode, slamming the door behind him. Wallace got to his feet and stared directly into the sun before bumping into a locked door.

"Hey, hey Herb, this door's..." Wallace jerked the handle a few times before it swung open.

***

It was a long drive home. I was bored. I scared everyone adjusting dials like an intern trying to prevent a nuclear meltdown. Jeremy appointed himself minister of dials and slapped my hand away whenever my fingers twitched for the volume, the temperature, the balance of treble and pouring silently from the speakers.

He found a station that broadcasted the work of Emmanuel Melchizedek Hutch 24/7.

"What kind of mind could invent heat and cold, could conjure thought and the endless plenitude of being? Is it even appropriate to approach something so utterly beyond our comprehension with the pretense of calling it 'mind?' Surely, this goes much deeper than mind, but what can possibly be said of a mystery so deep? Hello, I am Dr. Emmanuel Melchizedek Hutch, and I would like to ask you a question: Do you feel trapped by your addictions, or by dying dreams? Are you tempted to despair by a dying world? We can free you from fear of death. We can free you from fear of change. We can free you from fear itself.

"Sounds like the stuff we talk about when we're fried."

"We can free you from your culture, your creed, your tiny place in the world. We can free you from yourself. We can free you from your need to be free. Never before have the foundations of our civilization been shakier or more uncertain. When all other belief systems have failed, where will you turn for a solid

foundation to build a career, a family, a life? Join the largest expedition in America into that hitherto unfathomable gulf called 'truth' and you will find such a foundation. The academy was established as a mercy to humanity, to you. In these lean times, we share what we have with all. As a golden principle, our community accepts and cares for all who participate in our global work, especially those who may have nowhere else to turn."

"Dude, turn that off please," said Terrence.

"Oh yeah. I'm sorry friend."

"It's okay, it's jus-- I dunno, I helped him sell his miracle pills and his theories once he lost his shit and... I dunno. I guess I'd rather spend the rest of my adult life listening to my own thoughts."

15

Jeremy sat me down at his kitchen table once we got back to the island and told me he quit his job. His car was fresh out the shop. He was itching for a drive. He invited me along, saying he didn't know where we would end up or how long we would be gone. We shook on it. He warmed my numb hands and asked if I wanted any shroom tea. I scoffed and turned away, then agreed. He drew a little plastic bag out of his spice rack and shook it like a librarian investigating a sudden tear on an old folio.

"How much is left?"

"Well… I dunno. I don't wanna get caught with a scale. I don't think it'll be too much, especially if we split it."

"Okay. I think that makes sense."

So, we stood around working the material over with knives, a mortar, and pestle. We experimented with a style of brewing the caps and stems where we added citric acid during the boiling process. We stood still around our elixir as it steeped.

We were generous with ourselves, re-steeping our sacrament several times. We assembled a tiny flotilla of mind-altering mugs. We had taken great pains to gather enough lemons to completely prime our tea. We emulsified our watery fragments in juice and honey. The water seemed with a great confluence of influence. We looked each other in the eye after a pair of ostentatiously nonchalant nods and downed our mugs. It tasted fine. I'd been lazy squeezing the lemons. That or perhaps my hands were dull and heavy from being so fucking fried. Their seeds escaped into the brew. I spent a few minutes sifting them out, and this prevented me from drinking everything all at once as my travel companion did. Never before in my life had the change come on so fast. Within a matter of minutes, the safe and familiar album I'd put on became completely unrecognizable. His guitar leered ugly phrases, cursing the drummer and somehow myself as well. The bassist began to weep. I began to sweat profusely around my palms and felt transparent and numb. I went to lie down on the floor. As the port window of my kitchen yawned the abyssal deep drew closer to me.

"It's just fine... It's all right..." I reassured myself. "This will all be fine." I closed my eyes and sat still but all I wanted to do was run into it all and scream what was on everyone's mind: *Apocalypse! Apocalypse!* At once I was confronted by biomechanical visions of reeflike floridity. I had the lingering presence of mind to sit on a chair and gear up for the shitshow ahead. The faces implicated me in their twisted games of infinite age. I saw them play out in stages, seas of bones and jaws of iron rising and falling like the tides.

I got to my feet and was surprised to make it to the bedroom. There, lying on my drenched back, bathed in gray, I accepted my fate. I leaned back into the pillow as the sense of sedated paralysis manifested with another wave of cold sweats.

"Are you okay? You look about as sick as I feel..." Jeremy dry heaved and rushed out to hurl in the other room. The walls wept with eyes like the waving feathers of a filamental garden. The insides of my eyes were a sheet of singularities, each mirroring the seafoam glow of their neighbor. What remained of me dribbled over jaws within jaws within jaws, wombs upon wombs, to empty space. Words became marvelously transparent, comical as they were useful.

Then I felt myself getting sucked into a terrifying landscape of faces and machines mating with each other. The plumbing of my brain sketched itself out in a canvas of rippling gray tubes and glistening teeth. There was a serene and sickening beauty to the faces I saw. I couldn't tell where the boundaries between the wires and the sea of ink were. I heard qualities in the music that seemed to fit this horrible place. I couldn't separate what I heard from what I saw. I looked into my own mind and was disgusted at myself. All of this horror was within me, waiting to be revealed. I could feel my mind cannibalizing itself and thoroughly enjoying playing both roles. I thought of a grasshopper in a rat's mouth.

"I'm not even a concept." What does all that even mean? I laughed and laughed and cried and cried. How strange, to feel so dead and so alive at once! I felt somewhere between a moldering footnote, a patch of mildew on a shower curtain, and the endless sky. Somewhere in this blooming flower was a fish gasping at the side of the sea, a girl lying down in an orchard, a bald eagle alone in the endless blue, and there was me, the couch potato.

I looked out into the streets and saw the first leaves of autumn. The light caught them as they spiraled downwards. They made for pretty corpses in their reds and yellows. I saw the pervasiveness of death, the constancy of death, the inevitability of death. It really will happen to me, maybe in ten minutes or maybe in ten years. I once heard a preacher say that death isn't our natural, original condition. But here we all are, nourished by dead things, conceived and raised by dead or mortal people. Death, it would seem, comes before life, and it is where we abide after. Death merges into life. Life merges into death. No beginning. No end. They turn the wheel together. They are one. They are not. The branches of the trees intertwined with my nerves in a lattice of color and light. They were one, the nerves and the branches. They had never been apart. Their embrace was the marriage of time and motion, of the heavens and the earth, and of self and other.

I felt my lungs ache in my chest. They begged me to put aside the crutch I used to mask the real pain. But I couldn't stop, or rather I knew I wouldn't. I was ashamed of myself. My shame was killing me. I had to relent to the fact that if not shame, something else would do the job. Every step I took was another step toward death. There was no negotiating with it. Whatever words I had to greet it, I would likely not even get the chance to say them. There is no thought or deed so auspicious that it would free me from fate. I chuckled. In a way, death would take away my qualms and questions and soteriological anxieties without me having to lift a finger. The bare abiding truth that preceded me would shine forever after me. In that truth there is no blame. There is no regret. There is no need to desire perfection.

"I change my mind. *This* is the most alone I've felt in my entire life." I was neither one nor many and all the same a smarting welt.

"Are you dying?"

"God can murk me anytime. I'm not worried."

"Yeah but are you *doing okay?*" he asked. He began searching my pupils and searching on his phone.

"We are... Death... Do you feel it?" I asked.

"We are also... alive. You feel that, right?" I nodded at him, failing to comprehend what he said. "Just for my peace of mind, Jed. Do you have any symptoms besides all this fucking nausea?"

"All is nausea." I said, grappling furiously with the distinction between something and nothing. I simply couldn't come to conclusions. I could no longer know anything with any surety. The prospect of death and disintegration seemed as limiting as a parking ticket. Binaries mingled in an orgy of ambivalence. Come to think of it, I never did see good and evil together in the same room.

Realizing that I would inevitably lose everything, my health, my loved ones, my body, my mind, my life, my breath, I felt tears overflowing knowing that I would gladly lose it all again. Detached, I was free, and I was grateful for every tear. I was blind, to think of my problems as an enemy to my life, when indeed all that is would be impossible without the horrible, silent cruelty of impermanence. I saw its other side, the play of eternity with itself, laughter without end. Simple awareness, so mild and commonplace, in these moments shine with total brilliance, though completely unchanged. Unaffected by the cascading rhythms of cosmic birth and death, shimmering like light through a wave, mind goes its merry way. Beyond all frames of reference, the agony and beauty of life were reconciled. I lay face down in the muck of my own mind and gave myself up to end the war inside.

Nature was once a secret seed that unfolded into the present. In all its multiplicity it remains interconnected as it once was. I realize that I was truly part of this story. There was no longer any contradiction between my human and animal nature, nor between my living nature and the structure and organization of my atoms. There was no longer any dispute between my nature as something manifest and conditioned and the greater, infinite truth beyond. There was no more dispute between that perfect, infinite truth and the silence and darkness of space, its crystal clarity, and the softness of a flower. All the world's attributes spoke of each other.

I chuckled, doubled over, and drowned in peals of laughter. I've never laughed so hard in my entire life.

"What's bugging you?" asked Jeremy, waking up from a dream on the couch.

"Why nothing! Nothing at all!" I guffawed. What did it mean

that I no longer desired freedom? Had I attained it? Or left it behind? The mystery stayed with my smile a while, and there was no attitude of defensive, insistent wellbeing either. I just went my way.

16

And so, as September came, it went. Those sublime days belied the blustery chill that would soak us to the bone. The days got grayer, gloomier, and quieter. We cherished the temperate calm of evening. The waves reared as high as ever as the energy of summer withdrew like a happy dream. Terry finished packing his things at Eve's, who'd shoved everything of hers in the same boxes she'd come with.

She knocked at the door.

"Hello."

"Hi."

"Why are you here?"

"I'm... Jeremy's asleep."

"I meant... Well, we're leaving now, both of us. You can tell Jeremy so he can finally celebrate some peace and quiet." She stopped to look at me. "Be nice to him," she said as she stormed out into the wind. Terry looked at me like a desperate angel as Jeremy bumbled around in the apartment half asleep.

"Are you ready?" I asked. "I've got the couch all ready for you."

"No, the floor will be fine. It's bad enough you have to put up with my stuff all over your living room."

"I insist, take the fugly old couch. You've earned it." I smiled at him. He smiled too, tears in his eyes. He squatted down, wrapped his arms around his legs, and rocked back and forth. I held him for a moment.

"So, can I have the key to your place?" he asked. I nodded and gave him access to my home. Terry trotted off to my cottage. I stayed at Jeremy's while he got situated.

To help Terry would be to help myself. Were I to turn him away, suspecting selfish motives on my part, what would that make me? He tried his best to clean up my home, or at least his drinking, before I returned to stay with him. I had been steadily making progress, only drinking from boredom, or at dinner parties, or at parades, or at the bimonthly mollusc bake. Terry's drinking mushroomed into every aspect of his life.

He became a serious counterweight to my escapism. His drinking scared me. I couldn't bear to be like him, even if he was just acting like an earlier version of me. I assumed he'd heal soon enough and that everything would return to the way it was before he showed up in my life again.

***

There are at least two responses to getting dumped for being fucked up all the time. One is to live by the standard your partner tried to set for you, only after it's too late to prove that you can. The other is to get even more fucked up, having been liberated from standards once and for all. I think Terry chose the latter course of action, deciding to destroy his body as a form of revenge on Eve.

"That'll teach you to abandon the man you love!" he'd think.

He never used to pass out by the toilet or march around in public drunk before. He used to give me shit for that. I could feel my reserves of charity spring a new leak every time I'd come home to see twenty-two open bottles of beer, empty, shattered, or strewn around from some fit of rage. I saw myself in him. I did not pity myself nearly as much as I used to pity him. Everyone thought he'd sober up pretty quickly if he could just find someplace healthy to live. Under my roof he would drink anything he could find.

Sometimes I just smoked in the bathroom just so he wouldn't knock asking to talk. We'd go for a long walk in the moonlight once in a while. He'd usually be lit off his ass and I'd counsel him without trying to ruin his big shitfest. I stood by as he pitched himself off berms and shouted obscenities from lifeguard towers. Whenever Jeremy joined, Terry shrank back as if starved for attention.

Everything felt bad. I cared about Terry. He was a good guy. I didn't know what, if anything, I could say to remind him of the life he had yet to live. All I could do was sit down with him as he meditated or prayed by the beach or as he drank away his hangovers, anxiously waiting to see my own suffering in his and to see it healed. Perhaps then I'd be healed myself. Most nights I heard sobbing through my bedroom walls.

The part of Terry living in me demanded that I save the part of me living in him. Another part of me wanted my isolated and inviolable little kingdom back, as haunted as I felt alone there at night. I walked around with him to look at new apartments. I hinted, regrettably, how excited I was to see him established in a place of his own at virtually every meal. I tried to sound sweet. By a certain time, all my words just sounded hollow.

"You just gotta start loving yourself, Terry." When did all my pep talks turn into a bunch of platitudes? Seeing my friend sink deeper and deeper into misery my words of consolation seemed emptier and less original all the time. Maybe they were all derivative quips trademarked by some shadowy cabal of cold comfort. Maybe my mere mentioning of these hallowed phrases was going to earn me a visit from some righteous copyright agent with a gun for a face.

I have a memory of walking out onto the beach with him as the moon rose from the sea.

"Can you believe the decade's almost over?" he asked, drinking out of a solo cup.

"Can you believe the last twenty years? What'll it be like a decade from now?"

"They might be able to restore this place someday. Like, for real. With the crabs and the tidal pools and the other half of the island. Everything, Jed."

"Imagine that," I said.

"But when the water comes, when it *really* comes... No chance..." he said, gazing at the heavens.

Terry sat enthroned in my comfy chair, rum in hand and half-gone.

"I lost her," he slobbered.

"What do you mean?" I asked.

"She's leaving town for good. She left us both. She left us *both*. Because we're fucked, Jed. We are *FUCKED.*"

"Why? Because Eve's skipping town? Nothing's fucked!"

"We're *doomed.* She can tell." I sat down and caught my breath.

"Terry, look. I understand. It's awful. Just... I dunno. Have a drink and relax." Terry scoffed and spat in the sink.

"*You* relax. *You* drink," he demanded as he turned on me, so I did. We drank until our stomachs soured, anger forgotten forever. We drank until the only pain we knew was the loss of our basic motor functions. We slouched arm in arm on the porch watching people smoke by the canal when we could finally stand up, drenched in poison. Our breaths mingled with the cold. It drained cheer from my lungs. I felt fragile after a while. I wanted to fall down into a dreamless sleep on the spot rather than stand there another second.

"I'm gonna make some mimosas,"

"Mimosas?" I asked, slurring my speech. I felt off. I wandered inside after him and slouched, staring at a little painting of a sailboat I'd gotten from my family.

"How do you want yours? Strong?"

"Strong," I said with a grave vibe. I nodded to myself slowly, then I felt, for the first time since I was eighteen, a deep disgust for the taste of whiskey that shot through my aching gut. Nothing against that much hallowed breed of water, but in that moment my stomach and mind soured on the taste. I walked to the bathroom and pushed the door wide open. I bent over the toilet and felt like I was retching up my very soul. I went to turn on the light and saw a toilet full of blood. Oh shit.

I felt another wave coming, and it came and went, followed by another. I slumped against the wall and breathed heavily for a moment. I'd done it. I'd finally killed myself. I crawled into the kitchen where I saw Terrence pouring drinks. He deflated as he saw me.

"Terry, I'm bleeding." He wavered in shock for a moment. His eyes were fixed on the blood coating my chin.

"Do you need an ambulance…?" he asked. I stopped for a moment to think.

"Let's just get a cab or something." So, we got a lift to the emergency room. The driver seemed concerned but I felt I was beyond anyone's reach. I asked him to stop the car a block away from the emergency room and flung the door open, running out onto the sidewalk. I doubled over and sprayed the sidewalk with stomach acid tinged with crimson.

We were in the waiting room for two hours, maybe three. I got up again and again to go to this little bathroom stall, but after a while all I was getting was foam and bile. It kept coming, whenever I would take a sip of water, or every fifteen minutes.

Terry was worried sick, he'd bounce to and from the front desk like a nervous whippet.

"Wait here or leave, the decision's yours," said the lady at the desk. One man in a wheelchair sat silently for all those hours while his son read the newspaper beside him. Another man had been moaning that whole time, agonizing over something going wrong in his chest, from time to time shouting, "Help! Help!" I stumbled into the bathroom again and started hitting myself until I felt an uncanny wince in my jaw. It was a cry too urgent to ignore. I retched into the sink and watched as bundles of foam leaked out of my mouth into a piss-soaked toilet bowl.

"Stupid, stupid, stupid, throw your life away why don't you! Stupid, stupid, stupid, stupid!" repeated in my thoughts. I guessed at how short I'd cut my lifespan. What would I do with the rest of my life? I thought of being buried on the beach.

The emergency room happened to be a major trauma center. A man with a stroke came before me, a pile of men riddled with bullets were dumped at the front door and had to be rushed back immediately if their lives were to be saved. For all I was suffering, I saw so much more pain in everyone else. I thought of all the people bled dry by their time in the hospital, buying their lives with what little they had left. I shivered. I prayed. I cried. I called Jeremy and got no answer. His dreams were awesome and unshakable in their heaviness.

I shuffled back to the bathroom and slapped myself ineffectually. I contemplated banging my head on the porcelain sink. I threw up. A few hours in they took my vitals, and some hours later we got a room of our own. From there on I waited for blood tests, retching on a stool with foam coming out of my mouth. The staff treated me well. They recommended I see an internal medicine specialist and stop drinking. That's where I ended up that evening, offering up the sewage of my life much as I once offered rambling schrifts to my betters, passing myself off as a student of some kind.

From the depths of that excoriating trip the newborn morning said, "Do it right this time." Terry hovered around the bed. I could tell he felt bad, otherwise he'd have gone home to sleep. Eventually he said something:

"Love."

"What?"

"It seems so beyond belief, but that's the answer that confronts me every time. *Love*, it's how we got here. It's where we'll vanish. It's what we are if we are anything at all. When you're hopeless and it's all you have left wandering through death's gate, it will still bring you peace. As long as you love, you're free," said Terry.

"I feel you man. I've been there. But right now, years out and all I just feel like shit. What is love in all its wonderful… everything if we just feel like shit at the end of the day, y'know? What's it all fucking for?" I asked. I took a sip of orange juice from a dented paper shot glass.

"Love isn't a tool. It's something you can't escape. Tools are something you use. Love is different. Love is bigger than you. Recognize that and you might have a smoother social life. You might still get burned, but you'll heal faster if you find the power to forgive. The way love works on your fear of death, though, or any hopeless situation past any practical relief? That's when love means everything." said Terry.

"It's a little cliché though, huh?"

"Cliché? Is it cliché that life is full of suffering, that we feel pain? Does that make it any less obvious? Can you pull an obvious reality down and dismiss it like a tired dogma? You just can't, because love isn't an idea. Love is life itself."

"What about hate?"

"Love's shadow. We hate predators because we love our children. Sometimes we think hating others is the only way to love ourselves."

"What about the bird of prey pulling a vole's heart out? What about the wasp laying its eggs in a paralyzed grub?" I asked. At that Terry shrugged.

"Violent self-love. Love can be sadistic. It can be a horrible disease. What I'm saying is that without love in all its weird and terrible ways, the tapestry of life would fall apart."

"Self-love is a joke. I hate myself."

"Self-hatred is a cop out. 'Yeah, I'm shit.' Nobody cares, Jed. 'I hate myself' is not 'I'm sorry.' 'I hate myself' is not 'I care.' 'I hate myself' is not 'I love you.'."

"How can we love ourselves in others? How can we love ourselves without killing ourselves and the world?"

"You must empty yourself of the distinction between self and other. You must recognize — "

"That we are one flesh," I finished the quote. It was from a dead friend.

I knew what I had to do. It was hard to walk away from something that made good moments beautiful and bad ones bearable. I had to remember how many good moments the drink ripped apart. I had to remember the revulsion I felt for the tack-shop taste in my mouth moments before I heaved blood.

***

One afternoon I pulled into the gravel driveway and rested my head on the top of the steering wheel. I groaned and massaged my temples before going in. Terrence was meditating on the floor. I sat down and meditated with him, like we used to in high school. We surrendered to the silence that would reign over our graves, no more struggle, no more pain, resigned like ferns in a brushfire.

I opened my eyes as he did, and he said, "Herb reached out to me. I reached out to my brother. Rick is on board. He's already fished exactly what Herb wants out of the safe. He said that he wants to offer us real help. He knows our situation and he knows how we can help the Academy. He's gotten them to give us… enough to live on he said."

"What does he want?" I asked. Terry sighed, trying to think of where to begin.

"Hutch kept a manuscript hidden in a safe which he called his 'self-destruct button.' If it were ever published, that would be the end of his reputation. When asked why he didn't destroy it he'd just cry and say 'it's the only beautiful thing I ever wrote.' I'm sure there are plenty of people at the Academy who think it's some juicy blackmail or some forbidden revelation they can put their own twist on. If you play your part, I'll be out of your hair," he said.

"Anything, man," I said. I nodded, trying not to ask whether he'd found a place to go already. "You just have to go in there, take the initiation interview and pick up the file from my brother at the front desk on your way out. Herb's got liquid, Jed, he's richer than Micah. I'll be free to go wherever I want when Herb comes to Sassoon tonight."

"Terry, why can't you go in? Why do you need me?"

"My… Uncle is a very suspicious guy. He'd welcome me back but knowing him he'd probably slip me something before I can walk out of there with anything sensitive."

"You must hate that guy," I said.

"He just wants everything all the time," said Terry.

"Your family scares me a little."

"I'm sorry, Jed. I hate to ask this of you. I won't be able to protect you until I get on my feet and get another place like I had with Eve."

"Visit often. That's all I want you to do to repay me," I said.

"I will."

"I love you, man."

"Love you too brother. Tell him to go to hell."

17

In 1998 Emmanuel Melchizedek Hutch announced to a full Baptist congregation that he would be recusing himself from the body of Christ and starting 'the whole thing over again.' He invited all of his fellow cells to join him. He had taken the role of pastor at the struggling Second Baptist of Mill Creek out of the mistaken belief that the spirit was weak in the community and that the flesh would be willing. The rising tide of murmurs was anything but receptive. Heeding the vibe, he cut his sermon short by saving the announcement of his web-based drug portal for social media. His line of products, all reasonably priced, was intended to give his congregation 'real access' to the Lord.

"*NO. MORE. SYMBOLIC. HORSESHIT,*" he would say. Instead he said quietly that his intention was only to create a web of saints who might withstand one another's liberated glory through the shared pursuit of wisdom. Before Hutch could descend the stage's steps the Church's oldest member, Ernest Arnold, ninety-five, rose and outstretched a finger at the retreating apostate.

"*A FALSE SHEPHERD IS LOOSE AMONG THE SAINTS!*" he roared. Hutch shivered and turned and ran for the fire exit. Before he could get through the door Ernest was on him, warning him against triggering the alarm as it might frighten young ones. Hutch squeaked and ran out the door. From the beginning, each community he founded and guided was responsible for its own search for truth. To his credit, he always gave his followers the means to replace him with one of their own.

I tried to breathe my way to calm as I pulled into the reborn Millennial Congregation's parking lot some twenty years after that incident. I was a toddler when I knew this man. My father would wrestle him on the beach and lose. It was the only time I had ever seen my father lose at anything. Hutch had a habit of forgetting people and screaming at them for approaching him, thinking some agent was coming to tunnel into his brain. Long after I stopped seeking his company I had encounter after encounter with him. Each was more unpleasant than the last. I flipped through the incomprehensible prose of the Initiation handbook in preparation for my interview. Unspeakable truth indeed!

The Millennial Congregation was an empty husk of glass. Rick was inside. He recognized me as soon as I walked in the door. He strode up, six feet three inches of customer service.

"You've grown up so much Jed!" he said as he shook my hand and led me to Hutch's office.

"He's gonna pretend he's not excited but you're the first person to try and 'join' this year. Nobody even pretends this is a real religion but they're bonkers for the tinctures. Typical."

"So, uh... When I leave, I get the thing? From the safe?" I asked. Rick shushed me and smiled.

"Everything's ready. Just get through the interview and get back to Terry. We'll both be in your debt. I called Terry to come and get you," said Rick.

"Come again? My car's here..."

"Next!" Came Hutch's voice. Rick shrugged in some kind of apology and walked away. I stood there rubbing my fingers together watching the back of his head intently.

"Rick?" I squeaked.

"NEXT!" Hutch shouted. I swallowed my fear and walked

into his office.

"Hello Jedediah," he said the instant I swung the door open. As my eyes adjusted to the naked incandescent bulb hanging over his desk, I noticed his personal effects strewn everywhere. Empty crumpled paper cups stained with curdled cream-colored coffee, burnt out roaches the size of small cigars, an assortment of scratched, shattered, and beautifully maintained discs, tapes, cassettes, and books. "Sit down, please. I'm sorry about my… belligerence the last time me met."

"I'm sorry for insulting you. To be honest, I'm nobody to be criticizing anybody." Hutch held up his hand as if to stop me. He seemed ready to have whatever he was mixing, pinching at the sides of the bag, letting out a little landslide of powder. He examined his concoction and stirred it with his finger, and tried to deduce how many alkaloids he was about to put into his body.

"What's that?" I asked.

"How do you think Terry got his hands on something like Ichor? Sap, I like to call it. Do you think he got it from some sap in SoCal or however that little story goes? That he made a famous EP in one night? That's hype. Nobody knows who made that. He sold it to the Academy. He sold it around Sassoon. He was selling what came to be my parting gift to him: my favorite little helper stolen by the kilo from my own private stock by my own nephew," said Hutch. He pushed the pile of sap my way. "You want what's in my safe? I get it. I'm happy for Ricky and Terry. Good kids. They've worked for me, directly or indirectly long enough. But I'm tired of fuckwits at the Academy bribing my own family to steal from me. I won't punish them," he said. "But if you don't eat all of that, I will break your back over my knee." I gulped and looked down at the pile. I'd never seen sap in such a horrendous mass before. It seemed to clump over itself in webs of grayish clay. I scooped some of the powder into my mouth and gagged. My mouth went numb. "Is the taste all right? Want a little salt?" asked Hutch. His voice rang violently in my ears, like we were talking inside of an active microwave. I wished he would open a window. I began shivering violently in the lunar cold of the complex.

"I don't think..." I said, before losing my train of thought.

"I'll have some too," he said. He took his pinky finger and tugged a little corpuscle from the pile. He wedged it between his lips and his gums and gave me a big, delirious grin. "You have to finish all of it. You wanted to win my trust and cheat me, right? Think on it: I am letting you cheat me. You just have to earn it!" he shouted, rising from his chair. The incandescent bulb swung with the force of a flail as I fell from mine.

"Jesus, Mary, and Joseph..." I heard him say as he loomed over me. My nerves were beyond screaming. They burned like a forest. "I do wish I had put that on the label..."

18

Gabriela drank chamomile as she painted the best picture she could of smoking DMT in the Blue Ridge mountains to Eve. They were spending the afternoon in her backyard, by the treehouse she'd built over the summer.

"It's like I could see the intelligence of nature in front of me. I got this impression like, 'You think you know that you don't know, but how little you knew you didn't know! I looked down at my hands and thought 'you are fearfully and wonderfully made, you are fearfully and wonderfully made...' The sun and the trees and me fit together like some perfect machine. When I closed my eyes, I could see these flawless works of art... flawless... including my next sculpture."

"I'm happy for you. Your parents are off your back?"

"I've tried. They're a little more inquisitive about this sort of thing since Jed's... accident." Eve nodded at this and folded her arms beneath her head to look far into the sky.

"My parents couldn't get more 'inquisitive.' They already thought I was a fuck-up before I moved in with Terry. I never really knew what to do when I left college. I mean, I got the degree I wanted, I moved somewhere I liked..."

"I did what I wanted like you. I still do. I got into 3D art, you know, made my chibis. I was comfortable in art school like you were in Asheville. But you knew like I did that we could be happier somewhere else. Maybe we don't always guess where that somewhere is the first time. That's why you keep going," said Gabriela.

"Sassoon wasn't it..." Eve said.

"I was scared when I left art school early. Some of my friends were upset with me. I was upset that I wouldn't see Emil's first claymation thingy and... everything else was hoping to. I knew that my art would suffer there. I knew I would flourish somewhere else. I knew that. A few years later I was at this job with Jeremy working at a convenience store. I was happy to be selling former classmates' beer and cigarettes but we still asked ourselves why. At first, we're both wondering how the hell we got there, what we were making of ourselves. I had to learn I wasn't defined by... anything Eve, not my job, not anything. I resorted to the same shit that made me happy before I was eighteen. I was spending a little more time with my beloved family, making a little money, working with an old friend, and sculpting the fuck out of some clay. Sculpting the absolute fuck out of some clay, Eve. Last week I sold a sculpture of Max Planck eating a shoe for like - three hundred dollars?"

"Fuck yes!" shouted Eve, clapping her hands.

"Okay, monetizing my habits and all. But I'm doing what I love and my parents are finally happy I spent all that time chiseling wood in the backyard for something. If I'd listened to my doubters, I'd still be convinced that my only choice in life was between doing what made me happy or being a responsible adult."

"I guess my doubters gave me this mindset like this world that doesn't need or want more musicians."

"That's fucking bullshit. You said it, that's just a mindset. Artists help make life worth living. You are right to try to become the best musician in a world swarming with them. You're growing every day! Your songs are like getting hit over the head with a thesaurus but then you find out it's a pillow of cotton candy. That is a gift. You might think you complicate your life a little less by strangling your art but the opposite is true. Measuring our worth against these fucking one-dimensional metrics of success and all, like people are that simple. We can never be shown the full depth of who we are in art but every artist who abandons their craft means a loss for us all. We find ourselves diminished by the messages we get from art too often. You know that. I know that. And we're fucking awesome. We are change itself, growth itself. Don't you see that?" Gabriela said.

"I'm already feeling burnt out."

"When you get home tonight, sleep. That's what gets me through burnout. I worry about people. I'll stay in bed all day if I have to. Your brain has plenty of tools to heal itself but it needs the time and the space to do it.

"We are all so afraid thinking all the time that if we're not living up to our potential someone's gonna come to our door and walk around scolding us until the day we die. That was everyday life for me, only the scolding, stalking, piece of shit was my own train of thought gone off the tracks trying to steer me back onto them.

"One day I looked around and saw... basically everyone? Almost around me wrestling with the same deep, inner bullshit as me. My grandma and my grandad have their shit figured out. They're atheists, praise God. They have been since their university days. They were part of that whole existentialist thing, you see.

"They insisted space be made in my life for sculpture so that I could surpass their work if I chose. I asked them how they knew I'd be better at their favorite pastime than they were. Grandma said she didn't know. She paused for a moment before leaning over to me and saying being uncertain is exactly what we're supposed to be good at. Uncertainty makes us mindful of what drags us down and what we must cherish and preserve and hew out of the brittle rock with all of our strength."

"You are a very skeptical woman, Gabriela, more than we were. My daughter and your father rightly prize that because of your awards and your degrees. We prize that because yours is a new horizon. You will think for yourself in an uncertain time. Your care to release your truth from stone, to hammer away the noise, will make something wonderful.' I think when folks sell their brains out and have all their uncertainties removed, they're desperately trying to buy something they've just guaranteed they'll never have: stillness within motion. So, fuck even lying to yourself like some other person is gonna know what you need out of life."

"Yeah. *Yeah. FUCK THAT!*" Eve punched the air. She went for an overhead kick, a move she had not practiced in years, and slipped in the autumn mud.

"The fuck? Easy on the mud! I just got that mud installed… bruh… stop giggling and clean up this mess!" Gabriela collapsed from laughter.

19

I slumped onto my bed at last after a week in the hospital. I cannot and will not recount it. I checked my phone. No messages. I stared out of the blinds. I had coffee with Eve in one hour. I walked outside in my bathrobe and inhaled the humid, gray air of mid-fall. I smiled and turned to go back inside. I got dressed slowly, conscious of the odd stiffness of my limbs. I grabbed my wallet, keys, and phone. She pulled up in her new car.

"I was gonna meet you at the —"

"Jed," she snapped. I smiled and sat down on my wooden porch. I never heard the sadness in the calls of seagulls more clearly than I did that morning drinking coffee with the woman I called the love of my life on the porch of the home of my youth.

"Thank you, Eve. Thank you for coming back into my life. I think if I'd lived out the rest of my days without ever seeing you again... I would have regretted that. In fact, I'd go through it all again."

"I wouldn't..." she cleared her throat, "... I will never forget you Jed. You will always be who you were to me," she said. "Sorry if that was jumbled. I think..." She looked at me and looked away. "I warned you so many times something like this would happen."

"I know."

"And I'm happy you're not alone, even if it's only for a little while."

"Thank you," I said with effort. She drained the last of her coffee from her cup and grabbed her purse, looking intently at her phone. Before she walked off, I asked: "Eve, what do you think of me? Who am I to you?"

"Who *am* I? That's who you are." I laughed. Before I could think, another question slipped out: "Terry told me you were leaving town. Is that true?" I asked. She crooked her brow at me.

"You're leaving too, aren't you?" I shrugged.

"Yeah, I guess so. Jeremy saved my life. I go where he goes." Eve nodded. She thought about what she wanted to say.

"I'm at a place where I can be where I want to be. I'm lucky to have that privilege. If I have a chance to help other people and do what I want… I can't waste that chance. Really, I just want to get a little place by the waterway and *not* drink and *not* smoke and *just fucking create.*"

"Still gonna be drinking coffee?"

"Uhm… Yeah, I will."

"Now we know where you're still holding on." She smiled at me like she hadn't in years. "I'm happy you're happy," I said. I saw her walk over to her car and get in. She stood at the driver's side door staring at me for the last time before sitting down, shutting the door, and driving away. I breathed out and let my head hang between my legs. My fingernails dug into my knees and I began to cry.

I gently put my wallet, keys and phone on the table. I stumbled out the door. I had been told not to run anymore. My feet tenderized the asphalt as I charged down the street and rounded the corner. When my feet hit the sand, I collapsed and felt something give way deep inside. I saw the sun breaking through the clouds. I fought with the sand to make my stand again. I hobbled to the sea, homeward. How can water refuse water's invitation? I scooped up a fiddler crab up into my hands and showed him the waves from up on high and the horizon. His feet balanced gently on my fingers like so many little pencils finally worn down to the nub.

"One day, little fellow, the waters will come and wash all of this away. All of it. And what's left of me too. Perhaps then you and I will speak in more familiar terms, even if it's just silence talking to itself at that point."

I stood with him a while. We made the strangest of pairs, perfectly calm at the dawn of the storm. Me, a meat castle on bone stilts; him, a nugget of hunger in an immaculate shell. We watched the sunset die in our own ways, showered by rain. All was still in motion. I could taste eternity in the air. I knew I was home, and that I had never left and would never leave.

When the water reached my shins, I gave myself to it. The ocean reached into my nose. Thunder and dark clouds approached. Rain poured over my head. The waters stung my sinuses. The skin that separated water from blood would give way one day, like a right hand wrestling its left to the ground.

***

Jeremy and I had noodles the morning we said goodbye to Terry. He waved at us from what was my porch as we drove away never to return. I sat in the passenger's seat, idly evaluating the relative depths of puddles as they passed and smiling at the sunlight winking through palm leaves. The bad weather had strewn grit and sand all over the roads the night before and the puddles were a fine muddy beige. The clouds winked at me in their rich variety. They crawled upon the opal dome of the sky at play with the light of the heavens.

I felt his hand on mine. I knew that if I closed my eyes at that moment, I would be safe. The sun would shine, shine, shine, shine on. What a terrible thing, to care for this frail form as the first and final priority, imprisoned by love of self and chained by fear to a corpse. I could already feel tongues of flame climbing through my ribs to plead my final case to the open sky.

What was the way out? To accept it all. To accept everything and nothing too. I yield to what is shattered in me. I see the truth bleeding through the cracks. I am going to die. You cannot fight with a broken arm, and there are some things you shouldn't attempt with a damaged mind. Acknowledge the wound and seek help. If something is permanently fucked to shit, accept it. The boundaries of the self are perforated. The other is only known through the self, and there is no self without the other. To accept my wounds and let peace reign between myself and the fire that consumes me, yes, I will forgive and endure all gladly. I closed my eyes and let my mind wander to the Sassoon already behind us.

Jeremy rested his hand on top of the steering wheel. He side-eyed me and smiled. The great sky passed overhead.

"You've come back."

"Bit by bit. Where to now?"

"You're not going to believe this: Wallace found some way to settle down in Sausalito. Don't ask me how, I don't know. I just got off the phone with him. Are you down to spend some time in California?" he asked.

"It's far," I mumbled. But I was smiling. "Let's do it. I like sailboats."

***

There is a profound lesson in the reality of death and our accursed capacity to forget. Leaving the past behind isn't simply a strategy for coping with life. It is the inevitable course of nature. Save for the great library in the heart of every cell and the words of bards and poets mingled and confused in the glare of history, very little remains to testify of all that was. This forgetting is a kind of forgiveness, perhaps the most perfect of all. Matter lives and dies countless times but restlessly reincarnates through the food chain without complaint, a picture of unconditional love.

We are taught to make as much of ourselves as we can. In truth, we find joy in gradually, painfully, getting over ourselves. Our greatest joys are not in a frozen moment but in transformation. We are all in the process of escaping ourselves, bargaining with ourselves, looking outside ourselves, growing despite ourselves, dying to others, dying to ourselves, and dying. The day will inevitably come when the face that meets you in the mirror is not your own, not who you thought you would see. Quite often the mirror goes sooner than this season's face. We dissolve into the sand whether we are shed of the illusion of birth or not. What we cannot do is stay the same. To try is the heart of despair.

We passed through Appalachia. Beyond I could see seas of green and red oceans of rock. I saw golden valleys of faces drawing breath under an open blue sky. I saw a smiling traveler in my seat. I saw life and death and all that defied their distinction. I saw beauty and terror. I saw all the heavens and all the earths crowned in majesty.

It was then, after so long, that I finally remembered what my mother told me before she died:

"I will be the wind in your hair and the sand under your feet. I will speak to you in the songs of the birds and the hum of the waves. I will be there when you rise and when you fall. When you cry, I will catch your tears in the salt of the sea." When I was at my worst, the world, my mother, still chose to shine on me. The birds still sing outside my window. Though I was ungrateful, the waters still gave me life day by day. It was not the fragile, unconquerable Earth that had calcified against me, but my own heart against it. Sometimes the only thing to rile us out of our sleep is to get caught in life's brittle pincers and be astonished above all by their softness.

Afterword

In a time when most are convinced of our imminent extinction, many of us also find ourselves addicted. The root of the Latin present infinitive verb *addicere* is composed of the preposition *ad,* meaning 'to,' and *dico,* 'to affirm or tell.' As a verb it has a diverse range of meanings. It can mean 'to speak favorably of something,' but it can also mean 'to sacrifice, abandon, or betray.' We then come to the noun *addictus,* one delivered into bondage for defaulting on a loan in which he pledged his own person as collateral.

When our sense of agency is eroded, that is, when we don't feel like we have any real say in our pursuit of happiness, we are in a sense lost to ourselves. Driven by desperation we come to seek joy by any means in our helplessness by sacrificing our own bodies or our own minds if necessary. Anything to not feel nothing at all. Before we know what happiness, we could have achieved with what health, what funds, what life we have, we are willing to stake the lot on a risky bargain with something that ends up dogging us as a kind of Mephistopheles. In the spirit of addiction, it is necessary sometimes to make sacrifices of a similar magnitude in the name of restoring the agency that opened the void into which we toss our countless offerings.

I remember thinking to myself a few months ago, "Before what's left of my abscess ridden gonads paint the insides of a medical waste bucket somewhere in Colorado, I had better finish my story about North Carolina." You see, I had recently left the latter state in great physical pain portending the last two of a quadrivium of surgical adventures, and was losing not only memories but chunks of myself along the journey. What remains of North Carolina in me is a deep reservoir of words and their attendant wonders, and as I absorb Colorado, I am grateful that the world isn't just NC and the sea surrounded by empty space. Such a sense of separation from mother earth only makes it more sacred to me. I hope you will join me in remembering fondly a time and a place that will come to be forgotten in time, save for the grace and will of God.

As we walk on to oblivion, we find ourselves increasingly uncomfortable and hemmed in, perhaps never knowing comfort within the confines of our own skin. More and more of us are born squirming, even writhing in our seats until we find something that calms the noise inside, something that can reconcile what is inside with the outside we are conditioned to believe is something both alien and completely beyond our ability to shape. Do we continue administering higher doses in the hopes that our unendurable condition prevails, or do we recognize the painkiller as part of the problem and work to address whatever wounds us with a clear mind. I'm completely fine by the way.